Jessica fiddled  und her neck. "So lom would want to

"Are you out ated, slamming down her book. "Doesn't it mean anything to you that Mom and Dad were happy being together tonight? Doesn't that matter to you at all?"

Jessica sighed and shook her head. "Sure, it was nice, Liz. But it doesn't change anything."

"But this could be the start of their getting back together," Elizabeth insisted. "If you just leave them alone, they'll work it out!"

."I don't think that's going to happen, I really don't," Jessica said regretfully.

Elizabeth's lower lip trembled. "How can you say that? How can you be so casual about it? How can you keep trying to fix Mom up with dates? I think it's really sick!"

Jessica shrugged and leaned back on her elbows. "I just don't want Mom to be lonely, that's all. There's nothing sick about that. You're the one who wants to keep dragging the past around. *That's* sick."

Bantam Books in the Sweet Valley High Series
Ask your bookseller for the books you have missed

SWEET VALLEY HIGH

THE PARENT PLOT

Written by
Kate William

Created by
FRANCINE PASCAL

BANTAM BOOKS
NEW YORK · TORONTO · LONDON · SYDNEY · AUCKLAND

RL 6, IL age 12 and up

THE PARENT PLOT
A Bantam Book / August 1990

Sweet Valley High is a trademark of Francine Pascal

Conceived by Francine Pascal

Produced by Daniel Weiss Associates, Inc.
33 West 17th Street
New York, NY 10011

Cover art by James Mathewuse

ISBN 0-553-28611-0

Published simultaneously in the United States and Canada

---

*Bantam Books are published by Bantam Books, a division of Bantam Doubleday
Dell Publishing Group, Inc. Its trademark, consisting of the words "Bantam
Books" and the portrayal of a rooster, is Registered in U.S. Patent and Trademark
Office and in other countries. Marca Registrada. Bantam Books, 666 Fifth Avenue,
New York, New York 10103.*

PRINTED IN THE UNITED STATES OF AMERICA

OPM   0 9 8 7 6 5 4 3 2 1

THE PARENT PLOT

One

Elizabeth Wakefield brought the morning issue of the *Sweet Valley News* into the kitchen and handed it to her mother. "Morning, Mom," she said. "The paper's late this morning. I heard Tom throwing it on the porch, so I went out and got it."

Alice Wakefield, who was sitting at the table, drinking a cup of coffee, smiled as she took the paper. "Thanks, honey."

The kitchen door opened again, and Elizabeth's twin sister, Jessica, breezed in. "We're getting our French quiz back today," she announced ominously. "*Quel horreur.*"

Mrs. Wakefield laughed as she opened the front section of the newspaper. "You'll survive, Jess."

1

Elizabeth helped herself to a blueberry muffin and orange juice. It was a normal breakfast, like a thousand others at the Wakefield house. Normal, that is, except for the fact that Mr. Wakefield wasn't there.

Recently Ned and Alice Wakefield had been going through a difficult period in their marriage. After weeks of unhappiness and bitter arguing, the twins' father had moved out of the house. Mr. and Mrs. Wakefield had decided that they both needed some time apart to figure out where their marriage was headed.

Nobody knew how long the separation would last, and Mr. and Mrs. Wakefield had urged Elizabeth, Jessica, and their brother, Steven, not to let it interrupt their routines. So Steven, who had been spending an unusual amount of time at home, had gone back to the nearby state college he attended. And Jessica, to Elizabeth's surprise, had gone right on with her life as if nothing had changed. But Elizabeth—even though she had tried—hadn't been able to stop worrying about her parents.

Now Mr. Wakefield was busy running for mayor of Sweet Valley, which didn't leave him much time to work things out with his wife.

"Mom, don't forget that Liz and I are going to the campaign office after school," Jessica said, polishing an apple with her napkin. "Dad says

2

there're a bunch of envelopes that need stuffing." She sat back and took a big bite of the apple. "It is so hectic over there," she said, "but it's fun, too."

Mrs. Wakefield gave her a weak smile. "That's nice."

Elizabeth winced. Tact was not Jessica's strong suit. In fact, Jessica didn't believe in subtlety at all. She was wild and daring, and she loved making grand entrances and dramatic exits. Some of her friends called her Hurricane Jessica, and Jessica always tried to live up to her nickname. If there was excitement somewhere, Jessica was sure to be in the middle of it. She loved being the center of attention.

Elizabeth was just the opposite. She was quiet, and even though she often headed committees at school and was extremely popular, she didn't really enjoy the limelight. Unlike Jessica, who changed her interests almost hourly, Elizabeth knew that she wanted to be a professional writer someday. She considered the hours she spent working on Sweet Valley High's school newspaper, *The Oracle*, valuable experience.

Also, Jessica liked to date a lot of guys. No one boy held her interest for any length of time. Elizabeth, however, had a steady boyfriend, Todd Wilkins, and enjoyed spending as much time as possible with him.

Sometimes it was hard to believe that Elizabeth and Jessica were identical twins. But both were five feet six, with golden blond hair and eyes the color of the Pacific Ocean. Each twin had a dimple in her left cheek that showed when she smiled, and each of them wore an identical gold lavaliere around her neck. They were carbon copies, or clones, as Steven liked to call them.

In spite of their differences, there was a special bond between the girls. Being identical twins gave them a closeness that nobody else could understand. Elizabeth loved her twin sister and was fiercely loyal to her—even if Jessica was as subtle as a bulldozer sometimes.

"Mom, I can come home after school if you want," Elizabeth offered.

Her mother shook her head. "Don't be silly," she said gently. "I know your father needs help."

"OK," Elizabeth agreed. She glanced at her mother from the corner of her eye. To Elizabeth, her mother looked tired and preoccupied. *If only there was some way to get Mom and Dad back together*, Elizabeth thought wistfully. But with the mayoral campaign in full swing, her father hardly had time for meals, let alone working out a complex relationship. Elizabeth shook her head regretfully. The odds were against her parents patching things up right now.

4

"Come on," Jessica said, pushing her chair back. "We'll be late for school."

"See you later, Mom," Elizabeth said, giving her a kiss on the cheek.

All the way to school Jessica chattered about the varsity cheerleading team, of which she was co-captain, and about her best friend, Lila Fowler. Elizabeth hardly listened, however. She was too preoccupied thinking about their parents' situation.

Once at school, she headed for her locker. She worked the combination mechanically, opened the door, and stood staring into the locker, lost in thought.

"You look like you just spotted a UFO in there," said a voice behind her.

Startled, Elizabeth turned around. "Oh, hi, Win," she said, laughing.

Winston Egbert was a boy she had known since first grade. He was tall and skinny, and always had a wisecrack for everyone. But that morning Elizabeth noticed the usual impish sparkle was missing from his eyes.

"What's up?" Elizabeth asked. "You look pretty gloomy."

Winston shrugged. "Oh, nothing, I guess. Well, OK, since you *insist* on dragging it out of me—it's Maria."

"Maria?" Elizabeth echoed. "I guess she's still

pretty upset about her father having to drop out of the mayoral race, right?" Maria Santelli was Winston's girlfriend.

Winston nodded. "That, plus people are really acting snotty to her. She thinks her father was framed, that he never took that bribe. But people in school are treating her like some kind of outcast."

Peter Santelli was the reason Mr. Wakefield was running for mayor. The two men had been friends for years, and when Mr. Santelli declared his candidacy, Mr. Wakefield had been behind him one hundred percent. Then an anonymous source had leaked the information that a large sum of money had been deposited in Mr. Santelli's bank account. It could only have been a bribe, or so everyone believed. In spite of a quick investigation and trial, during which Ned Wakefield had defended Peter Santelli, the possibility of a bribe could not be proven. There hadn't been enough evidence one way or the other. The damage had been done, however. Santelli had dropped out of the race in a cloud of suspicion, and Ned Wakefield stepped into his place.

"But even if he was guilty, that doesn't have anything to do with Maria," Elizabeth pointed out. "That's just not fair."

"Yeah, well, whoever said life was fair?" Winston said bitterly. "And she was so excited, too. She really had fun working on the campaign for him."

Elizabeth brightened. "Listen, do you think she would like it if I asked her to help my dad? I mean, that wouldn't hurt her feelings, would it?"

"I don't know," Winston admitted, putting his hands into his pockets. "But I think you should definitely give it a shot."

"I will," Elizabeth said firmly. She took her chemistry book out of her locker and then snapped the door shut. "I'll see her in French class. I'll ask her then."

Winston looked hopeful. "Great. Catch you later."

All through homeroom Elizabeth debated with herself. If *her* father had dropped out of the race, how would she feel about working for another candidate? She wasn't really sure, but she decided it wouldn't hurt to ask. And second period when she got to French and saw how depressed Maria looked, Elizabeth got up her nerve.

"Work for your dad?" Maria answered, sounding surprised.

Elizabeth bit her lip. "I just thought you might want to help out."

"He wants to work for the same things my father did," Maria went on in a thoughtful voice.

She twirled her pen absently. "And I know my father really likes yours."

"So what do you think?" Elizabeth pressed. "Do you want to come this afternoon and see how it goes?"

Maria smiled. "Sure," she said. "As long as you don't mind being associated with me."

Elizabeth gave her friend a playfully severe look. "Don't even joke about something like that," she said.

"Thanks," Maria whispered. She looked away. "Well, I'll meet you after school, I guess."

"And don't worry," Elizabeth went on emphatically. "I know he'll be cleared soon. I really believe that."

Maria nodded and smiled weakly.

Elizabeth went to her desk, deep in thought. Between worrying about her parents, trying to get her father elected, and wondering who was behind the Santelli scandal, she had quite a lot on her mind these days.

The moment Elizabeth, Jessica, and Maria entered the campaign office after school, two people called out to them.

"I need you guys over here!" Amanda Mason, a pretty, young attorney, said, waving sheets of telephone numbers.

Another one of Mr. Wakefield's aides, Ramon Valdes, dumped a box on a table. "These envelopes need stuffing immediately," he insisted.

"Whoa! I thought you guys liked me for my charming personality," Jessica said laughing. She pushed up her sleeves. "I hate stuffing envelopes," she told Ramon as she headed for Amanda.

"How about you two?" Ramon asked Elizabeth and Maria.

Elizabeth looked at Maria. Telephones were ringing, and people were talking and rushing back and forth.

"Well," Elizabeth said, her eyes sparkling, "are you ready for the madhouse?"

Maria chuckled and nodded. "I think I can handle it."

Together they headed for the table where Ramon was piling up envelopes, mailing labels, and letters. In minutes they had set up a miniature assembly line.

"You could use one more person here," Ramon said, frowning. "I think Terry is here somewhere." He hurried off.

"Is that Terry Knapp?" Maria asked Elizabeth. She peeled off a mailing label and pressed it down on an envelope.

Elizabeth nodded while she folded up a let-

9

ter. "Yeah, he's been working here. He's really nice, but whenever his uncle shows up, Terry suddenly has the urge for some fresh air."

"I can understand that," Maria said dryly.

Terry Knapp's uncle was one of Ned Wakefield's top political advisers. He had been helping out on Mr. Santelli's campaign. When Peter Santelli dropped out of the race, James Knapp and Henry Patman had convinced Mr. Wakefield to run in his place. Knapp had a lot of influential friends, and his advice on political matters was indispensable. Elizabeth knew her father relied heavily on him. But the fact was, Mr. Knapp was not exactly a likeable man. His nephew Terry wasn't the only one who avoided him. Elizabeth thought he was pushy and overbearing.

"Hi, Liz," Terry said, walking up. He gave Maria a big smile. "Welcome back to politics, Maria. Sorry about your dad," he added in a sympathetic voice.

Maria returned his smile and looked around the campaign office. "Thanks. I still want to help out, even though it isn't my father's race anymore."

"That's great," Terry said. He looked at the pile of stuffed envelopes and made a face. "Somebody has to lick all of those, right? Yuck."

"You can use a sponge," Elizabeth said, and laughed.

While Terry brought Maria up to date on the campaign, Elizabeth glanced around, wondering where her father was. She hadn't even had a chance to say hello to him yet. Part of the office was partitioned off with tall filing cabinets, creating a makeshift office for Mr. Wakefield. In a moment he came around the corner of the filing cabinets, and Mr. Knapp was right behind him. The two men walked over to the table where Elizabeth and the others were working.

"Well, all hands on deck, I see," Mr. Knapp said in a loud, hearty voice. He clapped Terry on the shoulder. Terry looked uncomfortable.

"Hi, Dad," Elizabeth said. She kissed him quickly on the cheek.

"How are you, honey?" he asked. He smiled at Maria. "Nice to see you."

"Looks like we can't get rid of you!" Mr. Knapp said to her. "Well, now, we know that you know how to lose; let's see if you can learn to win!"

Maria's cheeks flushed in embarrassment. "I just wanted to help," she protested.

"And I appreciate it," Mr. Wakefield said quickly.

Elizabeth felt sorry for her friend. She couldn't

11

believe Mr. Knapp would be so insensitive, but that was just the way he was. She watched as her father walked to the door with the other man. They spoke for a few minutes, and then Mr. Knapp left. Ned Wakefield stood where he was for a while, lost in thought.

He looks tired, Elizabeth realized.

She wondered if he missed her mother or if he was too busy to think about her. Elizabeth had to look away. Thinking about it only made her hurt more inside.

Two

Jessica checked the rearview mirror for traffic and then pulled away from the curb. The twins shared a Fiat Spider convertible, and Jessica loved driving with the top down. It was easier to get noticed that way. She smiled at a cute guy in an oncoming car and then glanced over at her twin.

"Politics is pretty crazy, isn't it?" she said in a casual tone. "I mean, you'd never catch *me* running for mayor, but it's fun working on Dad's campaign."

"Mmm." Elizabeth propped her elbow up on the door and leaned her head on her hand.

"And you meet really interesting people, don't you think?" Jessica went on. "Like, oh, say, Amanda Mason, for instance. She's nice."

Elizabeth was staring out at nothing. After a moment, she looked over. "What?"

"I said, Amanda Mason is really nice," Jessica repeated distinctly. She grinned and poked her twin in the ribs. "Come back to Earth, Liz."

"Sorry." Elizabeth sighed and lapsed back into moody silence.

Jessica gave her sister an exasperated glance. She was pretty sure she knew what Elizabeth was brooding about—their parents. But as far as Jessica could tell, it was a hopeless situation. She had seen it happen so many times to friends at school that she was absolutely positive about one thing: "trial" separations were just the first step toward getting divorced.

Of course, it was a terrible thing to have happened to their family, Jessica admitted. But what was the use of trying to change what wouldn't change? That would only make them all more upset. They would be better off if they accepted the situation as it was and concentrated on the future.

"So, Amanda was telling me all about how she went to law school in Washington, D.C.," Jessica went on, weaving in and out of traffic. "She says she wants to run for Congress someday, or maybe even governor or something."

She looked over at her sister and waited for an answer. "Liz?" Jessica finally said.

Elizabeth raised her head. "Sorry—what? Who are you talking about?"

"Amanda *Mason*," Jessica said, rolling her eyes. "She's so interesting, and smart. And pretty, too. Don't you think?"

"I guess," Elizabeth said.

Jessica gave her sister a sidelong look. "I think Dad thinks so, too."

"Oh," Elizabeth said in a faraway voice. Then she did a double take. "What do you mean?" she asked sharply, sitting up straighter.

Jessica arched an eyebrow. "I just said I think Dad likes Amanda, that's all. She's just his type."

"Just his *type*?" Elizabeth echoed, horrified. "Jessica, don't tell me you're trying to fix Dad up with Amanda Mason. Are you?"

"What's wrong with her?" Jessica asked indignantly. "Not only is she smart and pretty but—"

Elizabeth groaned. "There's nothing *wrong* with her. But Dad still happens to be married to Mom, in case you forgot. They'll get back together, you'll see."

Jessica shook her head and turned the car down their street. "Liz, face facts. It's over. Mom and Dad both have to get on with their lives. I think we should just accept that."

"No, I won't accept that!" Elizabeth retorted.

"They'll work it out on their own eventually, but if you start messing things up with some crazy matchmaking scheme, you're only going to make it more difficult for them." Her voice was shaking with emotion.

"OK, OK," Jessica said mildly. She didn't want Elizabeth to get all worked up. "Forget it," she went on, pulling into the driveway and turning off the motor. Their mother's car was already parked ahead of them.

Elizabeth sat back and regarded Jessica in silence for a few moments.

"Promise me you won't try to mess things up, Jess," Elizabeth pleaded.

"I won't mess things up," Jessica promised, her eyes wide and innocent. She crossed her heart and snapped her fingers twice. "Remember that? Our secret promise sign from when we were little?"

Elizabeth smiled sadly. "I remember." But she still was skeptical.

"Listen, I only want what's best for Mom and Dad," Jessica said truthfully. "You know that. They're my parents, too, you know, and I love them as much as you do."

"I know," Elizabeth said. "I just wish you'd try to think more positive."

Jessica nodded. "I will. Believe me."

But Jessica didn't mention that in this case,

she had a different definition of what constituted positive thinking. She followed Elizabeth into the house and back to the kitchen.

"Mom's in the pool," Elizabeth said, glancing out the window.

Jessica grabbed a can of diet soda from the refrigerator and strolled outside. Prince Albert, the family's golden Labrador retriever, trotted over to say hello.

"Hey, Prince," she whispered, rubbing his ears. "Hi, Mom," she added in a louder voice.

Alice Wakefield was doing a relaxed backstroke, and she slowed to a stop when Jessica called to her. "Hey, Jess," she said.

"You got home early," Jessica said.

Her mother swam over to the side of the pool and hung on. "The design project for the mall is just about wrapped up," her mother explained. "I decided to give myself the afternoon off for a treat."

"Lucky you," Jessica said. She sat down in a lounge chair and gazed thoughtfully at her mother. Prince Albert lay down at her side with a contented grunt.

Mrs. Wakefield climbed the pool ladder and stood on the pavement, dripping. Jessica regarded her mother with a critical eye. Her mother's slim, youthful figure and blond hair made her very attractive, Jessica decided.

"You seem very deep in thought, Jess," Mrs. Wakefield said as she reached for a towel. She smiled and stretched out in the lounge chair next to Jessica's. "Thinking great thoughts?"

"Mmm," Jessica answered, automatically returning her mother's smile. But mentally she was racing through the possibilities.

Maybe Jeremy Frank, the host of a local TV talk show, would be a good match, Jessica thought. He was so gorgeous that Jessica had tried flirting with him herself once. She knew she was a bit young for him, but he wasn't too young for her mother. But then Jessica remembered his stunning fiancée and made a sour face.

Scratch that one, she told herself, already thinking of more eligible bachelors. Someone rich would be a nice change. Her mother needed someone to dazzle her with lavish, expensive gifts.

Mr. Fowler! Jessica thought. Her friend's father was filthy rich, and divorced. He even had a wing of the hospital named after him. He had always been friendly to her mother, Jessica remembered. Maybe he had always been secretly attracted to her. And now that her mother was about to be single . . .

But the possibility of ending up with Lila for a stepsister was a chilling thought, no matter how remote a chance it was. Lila was fine for a friend, but she would be a real pain to live with.

"Scratch that," she murmured.

"What's that?" her mother asked.

Jessica smiled sweetly. "Nothing, Mom. Say, have you thought about getting a new bathing suit? Like a bikini, maybe?"

Her mother laughed and smoothed her wet hair back. "A bikini? I'm afraid my bikini days are far in the past."

"I don't know," Jessica replied with a shrug. "You'd look good in one. And you could go to the beach sometimes to swim, instead of always staying here alone."

Mrs. Wakefield turned and gave Jessica a surprised look. "Are you trying to tell me something, Jess?"

"No," Jessica replied. She smiled innocently. "I don't mean anything."

Her mother shook her head as she sat back again and turned her face to the late afternoon sun. But Jessica wasn't content to let the matter rest. She was determined to spice up her mother's social life, and the sooner the better. Staying home, dwelling on the disappointments of the past, was no way to live.

Elizabeth came out to join them on the patio. "Hi, Mom. Hey, Prince."

"Hi, Liz," Mrs. Wakefield answered with her eyes closed.

Prince thumped his tail on the ground without getting up.

"We stuffed about a zillion envelopes this afternoon," Elizabeth said, sitting down. "Dad wrote a letter about preserving the wilderness spaces that still exist in Sweet Valley, and how he wants to protect the environment."

"That's nice," Mrs. Wakefield said. She didn't look at Elizabeth.

"Because he wants to be sure Sweet Valley stays as beautiful as it is," Elizabeth went on earnestly.

Jessica glared at her twin sister. What did Elizabeth think she was doing, playing, "The Dating Game"? Ned, Bachelor Number One, was handsome, politically active, concerned about the environment. It sounded as if Elizabeth was trying to show him off.

"He wants to work on a policy about homeless people, too," Elizabeth continued. "He's considering sleeping out on the sidewalk sometime to see what it's like."

Mrs. Wakefield sat up abruptly and pulled her towel around her shoulders. "That sounds a bit like a publicity stunt to me," she said in a dry tone.

"It's not!" Elizabeth insisted. "He really cares,

Mom! He believes he has to experience it to know what needs to be done by the government. I think it's really important, and I'm glad he feels that way. Aren't you, Jess?" Elizabeth turned to Jessica and gave her a beseeching look.

But Jessica didn't want to take any part in what Elizabeth was trying to do. She knew it wouldn't succeed, and it was just making their mother upset. She looked away and shrugged noncommittally.

An irritated flush colored Elizabeth's cheeks. "He really has great ideas for this city, and everyone at the campaign office thinks he's doing a great job," she said.

"I'm going inside to change," their mother announced abruptly. When she closed the sliding glass doors of the dining room behind her, there was total silence.

"Nice going," Jessica said at last. She let out a disgusted sigh. "You just succeeded in making Mom cry. Good job."

Elizabeth was biting her lip. "She wasn't crying," she mumbled.

"Close enough," Jessica retorted. "Liz, what exactly is the big idea, talking like that about Dad in front of her? Are you totally cracked?"

"I just thought she would want to know what

he's doing, that's all," Elizabeth said. She sank into her chair and closed her eyes wearily.

"She doesn't want to know, trust me," Jessica said in an even tone. "The best thing for her is to forget about him. She'll never be happy until she starts over again."

"That's not true, and you know it," Elizabeth said.

"It *is* true, Liz!" Jessica gasped. "Why else would she practically run away instead of listening to you blab on and on about him?"

"Because she misses him and she's sad, that's why!" Elizabeth said. She looked as if she was about to start crying herself.

"How can she miss him?" Jessica scoffed. "All they've done for the last couple of months is fight, fight, fight. She doesn't want to keep being reminded of how miserable her life was. That's why she doesn't want to listen to you."

Elizabeth leaned over the side of the chair and slowly petted Prince Albert's back.

"Liz, face it," Jessica said. "You're the only one who won't admit they're splitting up for good. I don't like it, either, but that's just the way it is." Jessica stood up. "And the sooner you stop reminding Mom about Dad, the better."

Elizabeth didn't answer, and she didn't look up. Jessica stared at her for a moment and then turned on her heel and went inside. If Elizabeth continued doing this, Jessica thought, it was more important that ever to fix their mother up quickly with someone else. If she had someone to fall in love with again, the pain would start to go away.

Three

Elizabeth sat staring at her desk after dinner. She was supposed to be working on an article for *The Oracle*, but she couldn't concentrate. From the bathroom that connected her room to Jessica's, she heard the sound of the shower running. For some reason it made her feel very alone.

She thought back to her argument with Jessica. Was she reading the situation completely wrong, as Jessica insisted? Elizabeth just couldn't believe that was true. All her instincts told her her parents were unhappy about the separation. It wasn't just wishful thinking on her part, Elizabeth was certain.

She put her pen down and stared into space. Maybe they were just being stubborn, she mused, each of them waiting for the other to make the first move. Perhaps what they needed was a little help. She was sure if she could just get them talking, eventually they would see they were still in love.

As a rule, Elizabeth left devious scheming and manipulating to her sister, but she was willing to do anything to get her parents back together. She tried to decide what Jessica would do in this situation. Jessica had come up with all sorts of plans for splitting couples up or getting them together. All Elizabeth had to do was use some of her sister's tactics.

Suddenly she had an idea. Picking up the telephone by her bed, she dialed her father's number.

"Hi, Dad," she said when he answered.

"Liz? Hi. What's up?"

Elizabeth glanced at the bathroom door. Jessica would be safely out of the way in the shower for at least another ten minutes. Knowing how Jessica felt, Elizabeth didn't want any interference from her.

"I wanted to ask you something," Elizabeth began, lowering her voice. "I'm really concerned about this, and I don't know who else to talk to about it. Do you think you can help me out?"

"Sure, honey, what is it?"" her father asked, concerned. "Are you in some kind of trouble?"

Elizabeth gulped. She hated lying, especially

to her father. "Well, it's just that"—she scratched the mouthpiece of the phone before she continued, hoping it would sound as though there was some sort of interference—"if I should."

"What? Liz, there was some kind of static on the line," Ned Wakefield said. "I couldn't hear what you were saying."

"I said I don't know how—" Elizabeth scratched the mouthpiece again and squelched a pang of guilt. *All for a good cause*, she told herself.

"Liz," her father broke in. "We've got a bad connection. Something must be wrong with the wires. I'll call you right back. Maybe it will be better."

"What?" Elizabeth said, holding the phone far away from her mouth. "I can't hear you very well, Dad. It's a bad connection!"

"I said I'll call you right BACK!" her father repeated loudly.

Elizabeth hung up, ran to the door, and waited. Luckily Jessica was still in the shower.

When the phone rang, Elizabeth called out to her mother, "Mom! Can you answer it? I just put polish on my nails!"

The ringing stopped, and Elizabeth tiptoed down the hall to her mother's room. She paused outside the doorway to listen.

"Oh. I'm—I'm fine, thanks," Alice said in a low, controlled voice. "How are you?"

Elizabeth crossed her fingers. *Please let this work*, she prayed. She felt bad about eavesdropping on her mother, but she couldn't help herself.

"Yes, that's going fine, too," Mrs. Wakefield said. She sounded strained. "How—is the campaign going? Right, yes, the girls told me. No, I—no, I did not—Ned!"

Elizabeth's stomach flip-flopped. From her mother's tone, it didn't seem as if her plan was working quite the way she wanted it to.

"Ned, let's not have that argument again, all right? I'm just exhausted—no—OK. Yes, I'll tell her to call you. Bye."

Elizabeth heard her mother sigh and hang up the phone. She turned to race back to her room—and bumped into Jessica, who had quietly come up behind her.

"What are you lurking around here for?" Jessica said in surprise. She gave Elizabeth a suspicious look.

Elizabeth brushed past her sister and headed toward her own bedroom. She had to get back before her mother came and told her to call her father. "No reason," she muttered. She closed the door behind her and leaned against it.

I blew it, she moaned silently. *That was an absolute wash-out.*

Her parents, Elizabeth thought, had promised the family that they would be staying in touch. But that didn't seem to be happening. There had to be another way to get them together for a little while. Once they started talking—face-to-face—they would remember the special feelings they'd always had for each other.

"I'll think of something," Elizabeth whispered. "I have to."

Jessica held her breath while Mr. Collins handed back their English essays the next day. The teacher stopped at her desk and gave her an apologetic look. "Maybe next time," he said, showing her a red D on her paper. Under the grade Jessica read, "See me after class."

Heaving a sigh, Jessica slumped in her chair and scowled at the world. She saw Lila Fowler looking over at her curiously.

"What did you get?" Lila whispered.

Jessica looked heavenward before she answered. "D," she muttered.

Lila drew one finger across her throat. "And you tried so hard, too," she said sarcastically.

"Lay off," Jessica growled.

While Mr. Collins began talking about *Ma-*

dame Bovary, Jessica doodled in the margin of her notebook. From time to time she looked up to watch the handsome teacher. Some of her friends thought he looked like a younger version of Robert Redford, and Jessica had to agree. It was such a shame he was too old for her.

"What would make a proper, conventional lady like Emma Bovary have a love affair?" Mr. Collins asked the class. "Here she is, well provided for, with a good position in society, everything she could want. Why would she risk losing all that?"

Sandra Bacon raised her hand. "Because love is more important than all those things. If you don't feel loved, nothing else matters."

Jessica opened her eyes wide. The answer to her dilemma was standing right in front of her! She could fix up her mother with Mr. Collins! He wasn't *that* much younger. A perfect match, Jessica decided jubilantly. Her mother had always said how much she liked him, and Mr. Collins always seemed very happy to see Mrs. Wakefield whenever she came to school. Maybe there had always been a certain attraction there, Jessica speculated. They might hit it off instantly. And it probably wouldn't hurt her English grade, either.

This is perfect, she told herself with glee. She

couldn't wait until she had to talk to him about her English paper.

As soon as class was over, Jessica picked up her books and walked slowly to Mr. Collins's desk. She arranged her features into an expression of anxious disappointment. She stood in front of him with her eyes downcast while he shuffled his notes together.

"Hi, Jessica," Mr. Collins began, perching on the edge of his desk. He folded his arms and looked at her intently. "Now, here's the story. I had to give you a D because it's only a D essay. But I know you've got a lot on your mind right now with your parents. If you want a chance to rewrite your essay, I'll be happy to give you the time."

Jessica sidestepped the issue of rewriting and seized on his lead about her parents. "I know I shouldn't bring my personal problems to school," she said in a meek voice, "but it's pretty difficult at home right now."

"Sure, I understand," he said with a sympathetic smile. "And if you need someone to talk to—"

"It's my mother!" Jessica jumped in eagerly. "I'm so worried about her."

Mr. Collins seemed surprised. "What do you mean?"

"I shouldn't even be telling you this, but she's

31

so lonely," Jessica explained. "She was married for twenty years, and now it's all over. She doesn't know what to do."

"Now, don't be negative, Jessica," Mr. Collins said gently. "Your folks might be able to work things out."

Jessica shook her head. "It doesn't look that way. The marriage is definitely over. And now my mom is all alone."

Mr. Collins stood up and started erasing the blackboard. Was he getting interested, but trying not to show it? Jessica wondered.

"She probably misses your father," Mr. Collins said. "That's only natural."

"No! She doesn't miss him at all," Jessica insisted. "In fact, she's really glad he's gone."

"Glad?" Mr. Collins turned around and stared at her. "Are you sure?"

Jessica resisted a smile of triumph. He definitely seemed interested now. She nodded. "Their relationship was going downhill for a long time. I think she's just relieved, if you want to know the truth."

"I don't know," Mr. Collins said slowly. He shook his head and went back to erasing the blackboard. "I've had a number of conversations with both of your parents. They always seemed to me to be a very close couple. I can't believe they won't work things out."

Jessica groaned inwardly. "They *won't*," she repeated, trying to keep up her pose of sadness and worry. "And now poor Mom . . . I can't concentrate on my schoolwork at all, thinking about her. . . ." She sighed heavily and shook her head.

Mr. Collins didn't say anything. He was pretty slow to take the bait, Jessica thought.

"Well, about your grade?" Mr. Collins said briskly. "What are you going to do about it?"

Jessica bit her lip. She wasn't ready to give up yet. "I don't know. Maybe if you talked to my mother about how I'm doing . . ."

"It's not *her* grade," Mr. Collins pointed out.

Jessica shifted her weight from foot to foot. She was really getting frustrated. "A parent-teacher *conference*," she said with heavy emphasis. "Isn't that what teachers usually do? We can all talk about how I can improve my grade."

Mr. Collins looked at her silently for a moment. Then he nodded. "OK. If you think that will help, I'll be glad to talk to you both together. How about"—he checked his schedule—"Friday right after school? Will that be all right with your mother?"

"Absolutely," Jessica said. "It'll be perfect. I know she'll be free then."

"You're sure?" he asked.

Nodding vigorously, Jessica picked up her

books again and headed for the door. "She'll be here."

She pulled the door open and hurried out into the hallway. Lila moved away from a group of girls and came over to join her.

"What were you talking to Collins about?" she asked, falling into step beside Jessica.

Jessica gave her best friend a sly smile. "About improving my grade," she said.

"Oh, yeah? Did you offer him money?" Lila said with a snort.

"No," Jessica said. She smirked at Lila. "There are other things in life besides money, you know."

"Not that I've noticed," Lila replied, veering off into the crowd. "See you later."

Jessica went to her locker and let her thoughts roam. If her mother and Mr. Collins did fall in love, it could have a good effect on her grade. That was nothing to scoff at, but it wasn't the point. The most important thing was getting her mother interested in someone exciting.

Four

"Hi, I'm calling to see if you're registered to vote in Sweet Valley," Jessica said cheerfully. "You are? Great! Ned Wakefield would appreciate your vote for mayor on election day. Thanks, bye!"

She hung up the phone and put a check mark on her list of phone numbers. "Talk about a huge phone bill," she said with a laugh.

Elizabeth, Maria, and Terry Knapp were on the other phones at the table. The campaign office was buzzing with voices and typewriters and ringing phones. Jessica looked around and spotted her father and Amanda Mason having a conversation. Jessica's eyes brightened. Maybe she wouldn't have to do anything at all where that potential relationship was concerned.

"Thanks for your support," Elizabeth said.

She hung up the phone and then followed Jessica's gaze. "Don't get any bright ideas, Jess," she said.

Jessica turned back to the table and shrugged. "I don't know what you're talking about," she said breezily. She gave her sister an angelic smile. "Back to the phones, Liz."

For a moment Elizabeth looked at her with obvious suspicion. Then she shrugged and began to punch in another number on the telephone.

Jessica smiled to herself. She had no intention of letting Elizabeth get in the way of her plans.

"Hi, kids," said a familiar voice.

"Hi, Dad," Jessica replied as her father kissed her on the top of the head. She tipped her head back and grinned up at him. "We're slaving away at the phones for you. I hope you appreciate it."

Ned Wakefield ruffled her hair. "I'll be sure to put you on my Christmas card list. Just give your name to my secretary."

Jessica giggled.

"Hi, Dad," Elizabeth said, hanging up her phone. "How's it going?"

"OK," he said. He pulled a chair out and sat down with them. He held a sheaf of papers in his hand. "I'm working on this speech for tomorrow afternoon at the mall. Can I try it out on you?"

"Sure, Mr. Wakefield," Terry said. "Go for it."

"OK. I followed your uncle's advice. It's about economic development," Mr. Wakefield said. "See what you think of this paragraph."

While her father read from his speech, Jessica kept an expression of interest on her face. But the truth was, she thought the speech was boring. In fact, she thought all political speeches were boring. But she didn't have to tell her father that. She gazed around the crowded office and thought about what she should wear to her father's inaugural ball. Something strapless and dazzling. Something alluring and sexy. Something—

"It's really good, Dad," Elizabeth said.

Jessica snapped back to attention. "Definitely," she agreed. "That's a great speech. I really liked it a lot."

"Thanks," their father said, smiling. Then he looked beyond them. "Oh—I'll talk to you girls later. Don't leave without saying goodbye."

He stood up quickly and headed for the door. Jessica, Elizabeth, and Terry all followed him with their eyes. Mr. Knapp, Terry's uncle, had just come in. He was shaking hands with the other members of the campaign staff.

"Who's running for office here, anyway?" Elizabeth muttered.

Terry smiled sourly and went back to his telephone list. Jessica looked at them in surprise. Personally, she didn't see what was so awful about Mr. Knapp. He was a big bore, but after all, he was their father's most important political adviser. And he was filthy rich, too. In Jessica's book, filthy rich made up for a lot of deficiencies in other areas.

Jessica heard Maria let her breath out slowly. She was staring at Mr. Knapp and shaking her head. "What's wrong?" Jessica asked.

Maria looked away. "Nothing . . . I don't know. I just feel that my father got put against a wall in front of a firing squad and that Mr. Knapp is still on top of the world. It doesn't seem fair, that's all."

"Well, he didn't have anything to do with it," Jessica pointed out. "He was just helping your father's campaign. Why should he get in trouble, too?"

"I don't know." Maria shrugged. "There's no reason why he should get in trouble just for being part of Dad's team. It just bugs me to see him, that's all."

Jessica raised her eyebrows. It sounded to her as though Maria wanted everyone who had been associated with the disastrous Santelli campaign to go down in flames, just like her father.

"Then don't look at him," Jessica advised,

picking up her telephone receiver again. She grinned at Maria and then punched in another number.

"Hello," she said when the person answered. "Are you registered to vote in Sweet Valley? Fabulous! Don't forget to vote on election day, and please consider supporting Ned Wakefield for mayor. Goodbye." Jessica crossed that name off her list and sat back in her chair to look around. Amanda Mason was sitting in a corner, reading a file.

"I'll be right back," Jessica told the others. She stood up and strolled across the room. "Hi, Amanda. How's it going?"

Amanda looked up at her and smiled. "Hi— Elizabeth?"

"Wrong." Jessica laughed. She pulled a chair over and sat down. "You get one more try."

"Let me guess—Jessica?" Amanda teased.

"Right. Listen, I just wanted to tell you," Jessica began in a confidential tone. "I know my father is really busy, and he doesn't have a lot of time to talk to people personally, but he really appreciates all the work you've been doing for him."

Amanda smiled. "Well, thanks. I really enjoy it. It's a good campaign."

"And a good candidate," Jessica added. She searched Amanda's face for telltale signs that the woman might be interested in her father.

"He has interesting ideas," Amanda agreed. "And a lot of energy and integrity."

Jessica let out a gasp of surprise. "He said *exactly* the same thing about you!" she said, shaking her head. "Isn't that amazing?"

"He did?" Amanda asked. She looked pleased. "That's nice to hear. I'm glad I'm doing my job well."

"Don't think Dad doesn't notice you," Jessica went on. She gave Amanda a significant look. "He does."

Amanda blinked. "Oh, I—"

"Jessica!" Elizabeth called.

Irritated, Jessica glanced over at her twin. Elizabeth was regarding her suspiciously.

"Can you come here a minute?" Elizabeth asked. Her voice sounded bright and friendly, but Jessica could read her sister perfectly. Elizabeth was saying, "I know just what you're doing, and I want you to cut it out."

But Jessica was not going to cut it out. "I'll be right there," Jessica said, giving Elizabeth an equally bright, friendly smile. She knew her message was clear: "There's nothing you can do to stop me."

"So," Jessica continued, turning back to Amanda, "are you staying late tonight?"

Amanda shook her head and looked over at the wall clock. It was five-thirty. "No, I have plans. My boyfriend and I are having dinner with his boss."

"Boyfriend?" Jessica repeated, her face falling. "I didn't know you had a boyfriend."

"Well, fiancé, actually," Amanda said. She stood up with a smile. "After six years, we finally decided to make it official."

Jessica managed a sick smile. "Congratulations," she muttered.

"I'll see you tomorrow," Amanda said. "Oh, there he is now," she added. A tall, studious-looking man is a three-piece suit had just entered the office. With a quick smile for Jessica, Amanda put the file away, picked up her purse, and went to the door. Her fiancé kissed her cheek, and they left together.

Jessica slumped in her chair and heaved a disgusted sigh.

Elizabeth walked over, a big smile on her face. "Did somebody kick your sand castle over?"

"What a brilliantly witty thing to say," Jessica replied sarcastically.

Elizabeth just laughed and kept walking. Jessica watched her in silence. So Plan A was on the rocks. That simply meant it was time to come up with Plan B.

Elizabeth drove home alone from school the next day. Jessica had stayed late for cheerleading practice, so she was safely out of the way. Elizabeth checked her watch and did some mental calculations. Her father's speech at the mall was scheduled for three-thirty. If she timed it just right, her plan should come off perfectly.

But first she had some convincing to do.

"Mom?" she called out, walking through the house. Her mother had decided to work at home that day, which also fit in with Elizabeth's plan.

Through the sliding glass doors in the dining room, Elizabeth saw her mother out on the patio with a pile of sketches and sample books spread out on the picnic table.

"Hi, Mom," Elizabeth said as she opened the door.

Her mother looked up, shielding her eyes from the sun. "Hi, Liz. How was school today?"

"Good." Elizabeth sat down across from her mother. "Mom, I need some advice," she began.

"I'm not the world's greatest authority on anything these days," Mrs. Wakefield said dryly. She smiled and squeezed Elizabeth's hand. "But go ahead. Ask away."

Elizabeth ignored her mother's ironic tone. "It's about a present for Penny's birthday," she explained. Penny Ayala was the editor-in-chief of *The Oracle*. "Do you think you could come to the mall with me and help me decide? I narrowed it down to two choices."

"Why don't you ask Jessica? Or Enid?" Mrs. Wakefield suggested. "Don't you think—"

"I want *your* advice, Mom," Elizabeth broke in. "I trust your taste more than anyone's."

Her mother smiled. "I guess I can't resist a compliment like that. All right. Let's go." She began to get up.

"Oh!" Elizabeth shook her head. "I have to do something first," she lied. "Can we go in about half an hour?"

"Sure. Just say when." Her mother went back to examining her sketches.

Elizabeth breathed a sigh of relief and hurried back inside. Once in her room, she paced back and forth for half an hour. She couldn't concentrate on homework. She was too nervous about getting her mother to the mall at precisely the right time. If they hit it just as her father's speech was over, it would be natural for Alice to say hello and ask how the campaign was going.

And then one thing would lead to another. Her father might even come home for dinner. All it took was just that first, carefully arranged, "accidental" meeting.

At least that was what Elizabeth was counting on. When she judged it to be exactly the right time to leave, she ran downstairs and got her mother. In just a few minutes they were parking at the mall.

"It looks pretty crowded today," Alice commented.

"Maybe there's a sale going on," Elizabeth said. She glanced anxiously at her watch. It was four o'clock. Her father's speech should just be ending. "Come on."

As soon as they entered the big central atrium, they could hear Ned Wakefield's voice saying, "Thanks for coming out today, folks. And thanks for your patience during the problem we had with the public address system. We've got it all cleared up now."

Mrs. Wakefield stopped in her tracks. Her face turned pink. "What the—"

Elizabeth looked around wildly. Why did there have to be a technical delay *today*?

"Did you know he'd be here?" Mrs. Wakefield asked in a startled voice. "Something tells me this isn't exactly a coincidence."

"Well, I thought . . ." Elizabeth bit her lip. "Maybe we should listen, since we're here . . ."

"Maybe," her mother said. She was obviously trying to keep her tone very light and breezy. "After all, I have to vote for someone. I guess I should know what the candidates stand for."

Elizabeth smiled faintly and turned her attention to her father.

"I want a Sweet Valley with a strong economy," he was saying. "I want a Sweet Valley that knows how to do business. I want a Sweet Valley that can take care of itself, that attracts business and industry, not just from California, but from all over the country. I want a Sweet Valley that will prosper into the twenty-first century."

Elizabeth glanced at her mother to see how this was going over. Mrs. Wakefield had a very skeptical expression on her face.

"I want, I want, I want," Alice repeated. She arched her eyebrows. "I guess I've heard enough. Let's go, Liz." She turned and headed back toward the main entrance.

"Mom!" Elizabeth hurried after her. "Wait a minute, Mom!"

Alice stopped at the door and turned. "Honey, I don't mean to be a pain, but I *really* don't want to be here right now." She yanked open the door. "I know you mean well, but you shouldn't have gone to the trouble."

Elizabeth cast one more look back at her father. He hadn't even seen them. Her plan had been a complete flop.

Five

After her last class on Friday, Elizabeth spotted Jessica in the hallway.

"Are you coming to the campaign office?" she asked as she hitched her book bag over one shoulder.

Jessica shook her head. "I have to stay after—for my conference with Mom and Mr. Collins."

"Oh, right." Elizabeth walked a few steps and then turned around. Jessica had a devious gleam in her eyes, but Elizabeth didn't know why. "What's it about?" she asked.

"My English grade, what else? You sure are suspicious lately," Jessica replied. She waggled her fingers. "Ta-ta." She sauntered off down the hall.

Elizabeth could tell that Jessica was up to something, but there was no way of knowing just what. Just then, Maria Santelli walked over to her.

"Hi, Liz. Can I catch a ride with you?" Maria asked.

"A ride?" Elizabeth asked vaguely. Then she shook her head, as if to dispel her thoughts. "Oh, right, Maria. Sure. Sorry."

Maria didn't say anything. She seemed as preoccupied as Elizabeth felt. They drove in silence to the campaign office. The whole way over, Elizabeth tried to come up with a new way to bring her parents back together. Everything she had tried so far had been a complete failure. Just thinking about the whole mess gave her a headache. She sighed heavily.

"Sorry I'm being such a moper," she told Maria as she parked the car.

Maria shrugged. "That's OK. I am, too."

Elizabeth felt sorry for her. *Life at the Santellis' house must be pretty depressing these days*, she decided. *Probably as depressing as life at the Wakefields'.*

"Come on," Elizabeth said with a sympathetic smile. "Let's draw mustaches on my dad's posters. He'll love it."

Maria couldn't help laughing. "I'll bet," she said. Together they walked into the office, which seemed to be empty. "It's quiet today," Maria observed. "Where is everyone?"

"Anyone here?" Elizabeth called out.

"They abandoned the ship," Mr. Wakefield said from behind the filing cabinets that partitioned off his office. He stood up and looked around the corner. "Just kidding. They all went to Secca Lake to get things ready for my speech this evening."

Elizabeth kissed her father on the cheek and put her book bag on a chair. "What do you want us to do?"

"Amanda gave me strict instructions," he said, walking over to a stack of cartons. "All of these things have to be collated. There's a campaign letter, a bumper sticker, and an envelope for contributions."

Elizabeth groaned. "I thought politics was supposed to be exciting."

Her father laughed. "Sorry. There's a lot of grunt work before you get to the thrills." He ran one hand through his dark hair. "I have to make some last-minute changes on my speech. Think you can handle this on your own, girls?"

"Sure, Mr. Wakefield," Maria said. "We're getting to be pros at the assembly-line stuff."

"Good. Let me know if you need anything." He walked off and disappeared behind the filing cabinets.

Elizabeth and Maria arranged the piles of sheets, envelopes, and bumper stickers in order, then sat cross-legged on the floor amid the cartons. Elizabeth felt like a little kid in a homemade fort. Just behind her, beyond the cabinets, she could hear her father's chair creak from time to time as he moved around.

"I'm thirsty," Maria said. "I'm going to go get us something to drink. You want a root beer as usual?"

"That would be great," Elizabeth said.

"I'll be right back." Maria headed toward the door.

Elizabeth began putting together the campaign materials. She quickly fell into a rhythm: paper one, paper two, contribution envelope, bumper sticker. It was very quiet in the office. She let her mind drift.

"How's it going?" her father called out after a few minutes of silence. His voice carried easily over the row of filing cabinets.

"Fine, Dad," she replied. She could hear him shuffling papers. "It's pretty mindless, really."

There was a short silence. Then he continued, "How are you, Liz? Is everything all right with you?"

Elizabeth stopped what she was doing and stared into space. Everything was as far from all right as it had ever been in her life. A lump rose in her throat, and her vision blurred behind sudden tears.

"I miss you, Dad," she choked out. She took a deep breath. "I wish you would come home."

Her father's chair creaked. "I'm sorry, honey," he said in a tired voice. "I know all this is hard on you, but . . ."

Elizabeth nodded, even though she knew he couldn't see her. She wiped her eyes. Then she went back to collating: paper one, paper two, contribution envelope, bumper sticker. She tried to make her mind blank, but too many thoughts kept intruding. Her whole life was reduced to one concern: her parents. Dimly she heard the door open. She wiped her eyes again so Maria wouldn't see her cry, but she heard a heavier tread than Maria's.

"Ned? Anyone here?" It was Mr. Knapp's voice. The door shut with a click.

"In here, Jim." Elizabeth's father called out. His chair creaked again as he stood up. "How are you today?"

"Fine, just fine," Mr. Knapp said jovially. "Say, I'm glad I caught you alone. Gives us a chance for a nice, quiet talk."

Elizabeth raised her head. Obviously he hadn't noticed her sitting among the boxes and cartons. She wondered if she should cough discreetly, just to let him know she was there. But something stopped her. She held her breath and listened.

"Sure, Jim. It's usually so noisy in here, I can't even hear myself think," Mr. Wakefield replied. "I'm just making a few revisions on tonight's speech."

"Oh? Why don't you run it by me? See how it plays," Knapp suggested.

"Well, first of all, I've changed the emphasis quite a bit. Since I'm giving it at Secca Lake, I thought it made sense to stress the need for some environmental safeguards," Mr. Wakefield explained.

"Ned, Ned—" Mr. Knapp chuckled. Elizabeth could picture his giving her father that superior smile of his. "I hear what you're saying. Honest. But I know something about this whole political rigmarole, believe me—"

"Of course you do," Mr. Wakefield broke in. "I appreciate your advice more than I can say."

"Then let me give you some," Knapp went on smoothly. "Sweet Valley is a good, healthy place to raise a family. We all agree on that. But people want to know they'll have jobs to support their families. All those other things come second with the voters, believe me. They want to know that the city has a master plan for long-range economic and business development. The other things just fall into place after that."

Elizabeth was beginning to feel very uneasy with what she was hearing, and not just because she knew it was wrong to eavesdrop.

"I just don't know if I feel comfortable with that, Jim," Mr. Wakefield said in a thoughtful voice. "The speech at the mall covered economic concerns pretty well, I thought. And since Secca Lake is a park, and a spot of such natural beauty, I think it's appropriate to talk about conservation issues there."

"OK. Here's the situation," Knapp said. His voice was still friendly and coaxing, but there was a slightly firmer edge to it. "As your chief adviser, I strongly recommend that you go back to the way we planned it before."

"But it seems to me—"

"All I'm saying is, my experience tells me this is the way to do it," Knapp pressed on relentlessly. "If you don't want to benefit from my experience, or if you think I'm just full of hogwash—"

"Come on, Jim." Mr. Wakefield laughed. "I didn't mean to suggest that at all. I just wonder if we need to sing this one tune at each rally."

Elizabeth nodded. She agreed with her father one hundred percent.

"It's what the voters want," Knapp said. "Foolish? Maybe they are. Limited, definitely. But all the surveys show that citizens vote through their wallets, Ned. You just don't understand that fact yet."

Elizabeth felt the color rise to her cheeks. It

didn't seem right for Knapp to be so patronizing to her father. After all, he was Mr. Wakefield's adviser, not his boss. She wished her father would tell him off. In fact, she wished her father would tell Knapp to take a hike.

"I think I do have a pretty good idea of how it works," Mr. Wakefield said quietly. "Politics has its own set of rules, and I'm more than willing to bow to your judgment when it comes to that. But I also have to let people know who I am and what I care about. This"—there was a rustling sound, as though he were waving the pages of his speech for emphasis— "this is something I care about."

In the tense silence Elizabeth could hear her heart pounding in her eardrums.

"Ned, I respect you for it. I really do," Knapp said. "But I have to be completely up front with you about this, like it or not. You've got a lot of support coming in from people who think those other issues should stay on the sidelines."

"What are you saying? I'll lose support if I talk about clean water and clean air?" Mr. Wakefield said in a surprised tone.

"No, no! Don't get me wrong," Knapp said. "Just think about it. If you're elected, you can do a lot for those things you care about. But you have to get elected first, and the people who can make it happen—well, you can't afford to alienate them."

Mr. Wakefield was silent.

"So, are we in agreement on this?" Knapp said, returning to his former hearty manner. "Good. I do know the ropes, Ned. You're smart to take my advice. So, I'll see you at Secca Lake. Knock 'em dead."

"Bye, Jim," Mr. Wakefield said quietly. "Thanks for the tip."

Elizabeth remained frozen in her spot until she heard the outside door shut behind Mr. Knapp. She felt terrible. In a moment her father walked around and stood at the entrance to her little fort. He sat on one of the cartons and looked at her silently. Elizabeth stared back, too confused and troubled to speak.

"I guess you heard all that, huh?" he said.

Elizabeth shook her head. "Why did you let him bulldoze you like that, Dad? It's your speech. Why can't you make it what you want?"

"Well, he really *is* more experienced in these matters, Liz," her father said slowly. "I owe a lot of my support to his efforts and his advice. I guess I just have to trust his judgment. I can't take risks when I'm still a newcomer to politics."

"It doesn't seem right," Elizabeth mumbled, staring at her pile of letters. "It doesn't seem . . ." Elizabeth tried to find the words to express what she was feeling. She had always thought of her father as honorable. But what was going on didn't fit in with her concept of honorable. It wasn't like her father to make such a compromise.

"Dad," she said, struggling with her feelings, "if you don't make the speech the way you—"

"I'm back!" Maria called, opening the door. She sounded out of breath. "There was such a huge line at the deli, I thought I'd die of thirst before I got to the cash register." She came around the cartons and put a can of root beer in front of Elizabeth. "Here."

"Thanks," Elizabeth whispered.

"I'm sorry, Mr. Wakefield. I didn't get you anything," Maria said. "Would you like me to run out and get you something?"

Mr. Wakefield stood up and headed for his office again. "That's all right, Maria. Thanks."

Elizabeth went back to putting together the pieces of the mailing. Her hands shook slightly, and she had to take a deep breath.

"What's up?" Maria asked, noticing Elizabeth's shaking hands.

"Nothing." Elizabeth shook her head. "Nothing, really."

Maria seemed doubtful, but she just reached for an envelope to seal. They were silent for a few minutes, and then Maria said, "Liz, I hope you don't mind, but I don't want to go to the lake this evening."

Elizabeth glanced at her. Mr. Santelli had made a big speech at Secca Lake, too. In fact, he had used the park as an example of what was best about Sweet Valley and what he wanted to preserve for the city. No wonder it had bad memories for Maria.

"That's OK," Elizabeth said. She took a long sip of her root beer then added, "I don't particularly feel like going, either."

Six

Jessica paced back and forth in front of the main door of Sweet Valley High. Her mother was due any minute. Jessica had high hopes for the conference. If she could just manage it successfully, she was confident her plan would work.

"Come on, Mom," she whispered impatiently. "Hurry up."

Like magic, her mother's station wagon turned into the driveway at just that moment. Waving, Jessica jogged down the broad steps.

"Hi, Jess," Alice Wakefield said as she got out of the car.

Jessica frowned. "Mom, why didn't you wear your blue blouse? It brings out the color of your eyes much better than this one." She smoothed her mother's hair down carefully.

"What?" Her mother laughed. "It won't help your grade if my eyes look nice, honey."

That's what you think, Jessica told her silently.

"I'm just nervous," she explained.

Alice Wakefield shook her head and chuckled. "Come on. Let's see what we can do about your English performance."

"Promise me you'll talk to him for a long time," Jessica said. "I have a feeling this is a really deep-rooted problem. So try to figure it out with him, OK?"

"And with you, too," her mother reminded her. "You'll be in on every gory detail. The whole point is that the three of us work it out together."

Jessica didn't say anything to that. But the fact was, she was planning *not* to be there. *Three's a crowd,* she thought.

At the door to Mr. Collins's classroom, Jessica paused to give her mother one more critical look. "Couldn't you have worn a little mascara?" she complained.

"Jessica!" Mrs. Wakefield shook her head in exasperation and pushed open the door.

"Ah, hi, Mrs. Wakefield," Mr. Collins said, looking up from his desk. He rose and came forward to shake her hand. "Thanks for coming."

"It's a pleasure," Mrs. Wakefield replied, smiling. "Well, maybe not a *pleasure*, exactly," she corrected herself, looking at Jessica.

Mr. Collins grinned. "Well, let's see what we can work out among the three of us. Have a seat."

"It's a good thing Mom just finished a big job," Jessica said brightly. "She's usually pretty busy. You know she's a successful interior designer, right?" she asked Mr. Collins. She was hoping he would pay her mother a gallant compliment.

He nodded. "Yes, I know."

"But I can manage to squeeze a few minutes for my kids into my busy schedule," Mrs. Wakefield said. Her eyes twinkled.

"I'm glad to hear that." Mr. Collins laughed. He opened his grade book. "Now, I think the problem here is a motivational one," he began. "You're smarter than you give yourself credit for, Jessica, but I'm pretty sure you just aren't trying very hard."

"That's so perceptive of you," Jessica agreed. She gave her mother an admiring expression. "He really understands human psychology, don't you think?"

Her mother raised her eyebrows slightly. "With all due respect to your teacher's understanding, it doesn't take a Sigmund Freud to see you don't care about your grades enough to make an effort."

"You're right." Jessica sighed. She appealed

to Mr. Collins. "She always gets right to the point. She's a real straight shooter."

"Which you are not," her teacher added seriously. "You seem to expend as much effort in getting around things as it would take to tackle them head-on."

Jessica suppressed a groan of impatience. No matter how hard she tried to steer the conversation off herself and onto them, Mr. Collins and her mother just weren't taking the bait. They both had one-track minds. She knew they would never really talk to each other while she was in the room.

"Jess, he's right about that," Mrs. Wakefield said. "If you put all your energy and creativity into doing your schoolwork instead of into thinking up ways to avoid it, your grades would be excellent."

"Take the last paper you wrote," Mr. Collins went on, leaning forward earnestly. "You started to say something interesting, but you didn't take it anywhere. You didn't push yourself."

Jessica snapped her fingers. "Oh! I left that paper in my locker. I'll go get it." She jumped up and ran out of the room before either of them had a chance to stop her. She slammed the door firmly behind her.

Out in the hall, Jessica didn't even bother to go to her locker. She knew she had left the paper at home. Instead, she crouched next to the door to Mr. Collins's room. Jessica wanted to hear every bit of her mother's conversation with Mr. Collins. How else would she know if her plan was working?

"I'm afraid she has always been like this," Mrs. Wakefield said with a rueful laugh.

"She's not failing," Mr. Collins said quickly. "There's no danger of that, but—" He paused. "I know things at home are a bit unsettled, and I want to help Jessica if I can."

"That's very nice of you, Mr. Collins."

"Call me Roger," he said.

Jessica grinned. *What an interesting development.*

"OK—Roger. I really appreciate your concern," Mrs. Wakefield went on. "I do worry about how our—family situation might affect the girls. Well, Jessica specifically. She acts as though it doesn't bother her, and frankly that concerns me."

Jessica rolled her eyes. Could she help it if she believed in getting on with life? *Get on with it,* she ordered them silently.

"I know what you're going through," Mr. Collins said. "I've been there myself."

"That's right, I'd forgotten about your divorce," Mrs. Wakefield said in a surprised tone. "You really *do* understand."

If Mr. Collins was ever going to ask her mother

out, Jessica thought, this was the time. She crossed her fingers and hoped he didn't blow it.

"Listen, why don't we get together sometime? You could probably use a friend right now," Mr. Collins said warmly. "It would do you good to take your mind off things for a while and just enjoy yourself."

Mrs. Wakefield laughed. "Are you asking me for a date, Roger?"

"Well, I wouldn't put it in those terms," he replied warmly. "Just two people going out to dinner and sharing some friendly conversation."

"Actually, that sounds wonderful," Mrs. Wakefield said.

Jessica could picture Mr. Collins grinning. "How about tomorrow night at Chez Sam?" he suggested.

"OK," Mrs. Wakefield agreed. "I'm looking forward to it."

Jessica could tell from the tone of the conversation that neither one of them had any romantic intentions. But there was time for that.

Jessica pushed open the door. "I'm really sorry. I thought the paper was in my locker, but I guess I left it at home."

As she talked, she stole a quick glance at their expressions. They both seemed perfectly relaxed and at ease, not at all secretive. That confirmed her suspicion that they didn't see their date as romantic.

"But I was thinking about what you both said," she went on earnestly. "And I'm going to try harder. This little talk really straightened me out."

Her mother's expression was skeptical. "Really?" she asked.

"Really, Mom," Jessica said. She opened her eyes wide and nodded. "You both just put it all into perspective for me."

Mrs. Wakefield and Mr. Collins exchanged a doubtful look. But Mrs. Wakefield shrugged. "Well, in that case . . ."

"I guess that takes care of it," Jessica said cheerfully. She smiled at Mr. Collins. "Thanks a lot. I really appreciate what you've done."

"Don't mention it," he replied.

Jessica stood up and looked at her mother. Mrs. Wakefield rose. "OK. Let's go home."

Wearily Elizabeth walked down the upstairs hallway to her bedroom. Todd would be coming by later so they could go to a movie together, but she didn't feel very much like going out. Her experience at the campaign office had left her in a bad mood.

"Hi, Liz," Jessica said, appearing in the bathroom doorway. She was towel-drying her hair. "How did it go this afternoon?"

"OK," Elizabeth said evasively. She flopped onto her bed and stared at the ceiling. "Oh, before I forget, Dad wants to take us out to dinner tomorrow night. To Chez Sam."

"*What?*" Jessica shrieked.

Elizabeth raised her head to look at her twin. Jessica had a strange expression on her face. "Dad's taking us to Chez Sam tomorrow night," Elizabeth repeated. "Why? What's wrong with that?"

"Well . . . it's just . . . you know how crowded it always gets there," Jessica said, waving her arms dramatically. "We'd never get a reservation."

"Don't worry. Dad already has the reservation," Elizabeth told her. "It's all taken care of."

"Oh." Jessica frowned. "But what if I already have plans? I mean, Dad really has his nerve assuming I'm free on a Saturday night."

Elizabeth couldn't believe her sister's attitude. "Jess, this is Dad we're talking about. Remember him? He wants to take us out to dinner because he wants to spend some time with us away from the campaign office. If it's just another dumb party or something, it seems like you could skip it this time."

"Yeah, but . . ." Jessica fiddled with the doorknob. "But why does it have to be Chez Sam? I hate that place. The food is so snobbish."

"Snobbish? Jessica, you're cracking up," Elizabeth said in a mystified voice. "Last week you told Dad you love that place because it's so sophisticated! That's why he picked it, because he thought you really wanted to go there." Elizabeth was used to strange, unaccountable behavior from her twin, but this was just too odd. Something fishy was going on.

"Well, if he wanted to pick a place I like, I could tell him tons of other restaurants," Jessica said. "There's Guido's, the Carousel—"

Elizabeth closed her eyes and fell backward onto her bed. She didn't know what had gotten into Jessica, but now that she thought about it, she didn't really care. She wasn't in the mood to worry about her twin's strange obsession.

"Jessica," she began in as patient a voice as she could manage, "we're going to Chez Sam because that's where Dad wants to take us. I don't want to talk about it anymore. That's just the way it is. Period."

"Yeah, but—"

"Jessica!" Elizabeth gave her sister a warning look.

"All right, all right," Jessica said. She closed the bathroom door.

"You're weird, Wakefield!" Elizabeth called after her.

Seven

Elizabeth checked her reflection in her bedroom mirror. Behind her, she could see Jessica pacing nervously back and forth, twisting a strand of hair in her fingers.

"Maybe we should go to the new restaurant on Pacific Avenue," Jessica said. "Don't you think?"

Elizabeth carefully rubbed a smudge of eyeliner from her lower lid and said nothing.

Jessica made a sour face.

"Did Mom leave while I was in the shower?" Elizabeth asked, to change the subject.

Jessica stared at her as though Elizabeth had just suggested dyeing her hair green. "What do you mean?"

"I didn't know Mom was going out, that's

all," Elizabeth replied. She eyed Jessica skeptically. "What is wrong with you, anyway?"

"Nothing," Jessica said. She gave Elizabeth a fake smile and shrugged. "Nothing's wrong with me, Liz. Where *is* Dad, anyway? Maybe he forgot, and we won't have to go."

Elizabeth shook her head in defeat. "Unbelievable," she muttered. Then she heard a car stop out front. She looked out her bedroom window. "There he is. Come on."

She grabbed her purse and headed downstairs, with Jessica following slowly behind. Elizabeth went to the front closet and grabbed her blazer.

"Whoops! I left my jacket upstairs," Jessica exclaimed.

Elizabeth rolled her eyes. "Well, hurry up, will you?" She put her blazer on. "I'm going out to the car. I'll tell Dad you'll be out in a minute. And don't forget to lock the door."

"I'll be right out," Jessica promised.

Elizabeth grabbed her shoulder bag and headed out of the house to her father's car.

"Hi, Dad," she said, sliding into the front seat.

"Hi, sweetie," Mr. Wakefield replied. He kissed her cheek. "Where's Jess?"

"Coming," Elizabeth said. "And listen, whatever she says tonight, just ignore her, OK? She's acting like an alien took over her brain again."

"Again?" Mr. Wakefield teased. He glanced past her to the house. "Here she comes."

Jessica scrambled into the backseat. "Hi, Dad," she began. "You know, I was thinking—"

"Here we go," Elizabeth whispered.

Mr. Wakefield pulled out into the quiet street. "What, Jess?"

"Well, about Chez Sam," Jessica said. "You don't have to take us to such a fancy place, you know. I mean, it's just us, right?"

"Nothing's too good for my girls," their father said gallantly. "I want to take you there as a special treat."

"But, you know," Jessica went on, leaning forward between them, "there's this new place over on Pacific Avenue. The Leeward Isles. It's supposed to be really nice, Dad. That would be a special treat, too. Why don't we try it?"

"Next time," he said. "I can already taste the scallops in cream sauce I had last time I was at Chez Sam. I'd go into shock if my system didn't get them."

"I bet they have scallops at the Leeward Isles," Jessica persisted.

Elizabeth caught her father's eye. "See what I mean?" she said. "Alien mind control."

"That's our Jessica." Mr. Wakefield laughed.

For the rest of the drive Elizabeth and her father talked about the campaign. Jessica was silent.

When they arrived at Chez Sam, Jessica trudged behind the others to the entrance. She closed her eyes for a second, took a deep breath, and then followed them in.

"Ah, Mr. Wakefield!" the maître d' exclaimed as they entered. He picked up some menus. "Mrs. Wakefield is already here."

Elizabeth's stomach did a swan dive. She turned around slowly and gave her sister a dirty look.

"I'm sorry," Mr. Wakefield said, obviously confused. "I just have a table for three—myself and my daughters."

"Of course," the maître d' said smoothly. "Right this way."

Elizabeth let her father go first. She grabbed Jessica's arm. "What did you do?" she hissed angrily. "Who did you fix Mom up with?"

"You'll see," Jessica mumbled. She pulled her arm free and hurried after their father.

Elizabeth drew a deep breath. This explained Jessica's strange aversion to eating dinner at Chez Sam. As soon as she turned the corner into the dining room, Elizabeth saw her mother— and Mr. Collins. She was so surprised and em-

72

barrassed, she didn't even know if she should say hello to them. Averting her gaze, she followed her father and Jessica to their table. She hoped her father hadn't noticed. But no such luck.

"Well, this is unexpected," Mr. Wakefield said mildly.

Jessica let out a feeble laugh. "It sure is."

Elizabeth glanced at her mother as she sat down. Mrs. Wakefield was looking over at them, an expression of surprise on her face. Mr. Collins turned around and saw them, and his eyes widened.

"I don't mind going somewhere else, Dad," Elizabeth said in a choked voice. "I don't care."

"Don't be ridiculous, Liz," Mr. Wakefield replied. He looked at his menu and smiled. "We came here for dinner. Just because there are other people in the restaurant doesn't mean we can't have a good time."

"But, Dad—" Elizabeth broke off in confusion. She met her sister's glance and looked daggers at her.

Jessica smiled back innocently. Obviously, if their father wasn't upset, Jessica wasn't in trouble. She looked as happy as could be. She lifted her water glass and took a sip.

Furious, Elizabeth flicked open her napkin and put it in her lap.

"I know what I want," Mr. Wakefield said in an amused voice. "I think I'll have a Caesar salad with the scallops. How about you, Liz?"

Elizabeth looked at him mutely. She couldn't imagine eating anything. She didn't even pick up her menu.

"You like the orange chicken, don't you?" her father prompted. He smiled. "Or why don't you try the filet mignon?"

"I think I'll have the lobster tail," Jessica announced. "Plus caviar to start with. And chocolate mousse for dessert."

Mr. Wakefield's dark brown eyes were sparkling. "Would you like to reconsider, Miss Sophisticate?"

"Well, maybe not caviar," Jessica decided with a grin. "It's too salty, anyway. I'll just have the lobster and a salad."

"I thought you would see it my way," Mr. Wakefield teased. "Political candidates aren't exactly made of money, you know."

"No?" Jessica said, pretending to be disappointed. "What good is being a politician if you can't get something out of it?"

Elizabeth finally picked up her menu, but she stared at it unseeingly. How could they joke around when they knew who was sitting just a few tables away? "I'll have the orange chicken," she said finally.

"And root beer," her father added. "Let's see if we can get them to put it in a champagne glass." He beckoned to the waiter and ordered for them.

Jessica's smile was growing wider. She seemed perfectly happy to enjoy a fancy dinner now that she was out of danger.

"Mr. Wakefield," the maître d' said, stopping at their table, "there is a phone call for you, sir."

Elizabeth watched her father make his way through the dining room. Then she turned to her sister. "*What* are you doing?"

"Having a drink of water," Jessica said with a maddening smile. She lifted her glass and gazed at Elizabeth over the rim while she drank.

"You know what I mean," Elizabeth growled. "This is something you cooked up, I know it. What is Mom doing here with *Mr. Collins*?" Her voice rose.

Jessica rolled her eyes. "Keep your voice down, Liz, and relax. You're the only one who's worried about it. If Mom and Dad don't care, why should you?"

"That's not the point, Jessica," Elizabeth retorted. "You promised you weren't going to meddle. *This* is definitely meddling."

"Here comes Dad," Jessica said, "so let's drop it, OK?"

Elizabeth tried to control her emotions. She stole a quick glance at her mother as her father sat down. Mrs. Wakefield smiled sheepishly.

"Your mother seems to be having a nice time," Mr. Wakefield said.

"Dad . . ." Elizabeth began.

He looked over at Alice and Mr. Collins and, smiling, raised his glass to them.

Elizabeth's mother hesitated for a moment, then lifted her glass to return the toast. She appeared to be a little flustered, but there was a tiny smile on her face, too. Mr. Wakefield chuckled. Mrs. Wakefield said something to Mr. Collins, and they both stood up.

What is going on? Elizabeth wondered. They were heading straight for the twins and Mr. Wakefield. Elizabeth felt trapped.

"Hi, Mom," Jessica said in a cheerful voice. "Hi, Mr. Collins."

"How are you, Ned?" Mrs. Wakefield asked. Her smile was genuine. She put her hand on Elizabeth's shoulder and gave it a gentle, reassuring squeeze, as if to say "Don't worry."

"Why don't you join us?" Mr. Wakefield asked. He gave Mr. Collins a friendly smile. "It's not a private party."

Mr. Collins looked at Alice with a question in his eyes.

"What do you think, Roger? Should we get the waiter to move us over here?"

Elizabeth was shocked. Of all the possible scenarios, this was the most unexpected. Her parents were about to have dinner together, and she had Jessica to thank for it!

"Here, let's get some chairs," Mr. Wakefield said, standing up. A waiter hurried over, and explanations were made. In moments the table for three was a table for five.

"How's the campaign going?" Mr. Collins asked as soon as they were settled. "I wanted to come hear one of your speeches, but I haven't been able to make it so far."

"It's hard work, but I'm enjoying it," Mr. Wakefield answered. "Well, scratch that—I'm too busy to enjoy anything, but I like being absorbed this way. It's a real challenge, and I like that."

"Yeah, but you might keel over from exhaustion before election day," Jessica pointed out.

Elizabeth nodded. "Two more weeks and then—"

"If you win, you don't even get to catch your breath," Alice said.

"But who says I'm going to win?" Ned said playfully. "The voters are unpredictable."

"I hope they know a decent man when they

see one," Mrs. Wakefield said in an indignant tone. "They'd have to be either crazy or stupid not to vote for you."

Elizabeth's heart skipped a beat. What did her mother mean by that remark? And what about all those smiles going around the table? Had her parents reached a turning point right before her eyes? The more they all talked, the more she began to believe that they might actually get back together.

When the food came, Elizabeth was too nervous to eat. Throughout dinner she watched her parents like a hawk. It wasn't her imagination: She was sure they were getting along just the way they used to. But with Mr. Collins there, it was a bit awkward.

"We were planning to catch a nine o'clock movie," Mr. Collins said after they had paid the check. "Why don't we all go?"

Elizabeth looked at her father.

"Sorry, I still have work to do tonight," Ned replied. He smiled at Alice. "It was nice to see you."

She smiled and nodded. "Bye, Ned. Let's talk during the week and catch up a bit, OK? See you at home, girls."

Mr. Collins gave them all a warm smile. Then he and Mrs. Wakefield left together.

"Well, let's get going," Mr. Wakefield said.

Elizabeth kept her gaze on the floor. She was afraid her disappointment was written all over her face. It would have been wonderful for her parents to go to the movies together, even with Mr. Collins there.

"Mr. Collins is so nice, isn't he?" Jessica asked in the car. "He's a really good sport, too. I mean, he didn't have to—"

"What time is it?" Elizabeth interrupted loudly. She didn't want her sister to bring up *anything* about the evening.

"Quarter to nine," her father said, concentrating on the traffic.

Elizabeth remained silent for the rest of the ride while Jessica chattered on about school and cheerleading. When they stopped outside the house, Elizabeth held her breath.

"I'll call you tomorrow, girls," Mr. Wakefield said. The engine was still running.

Elizabeth swallowed hard and tried to smile. She had been hoping her father would come in with them. "OK, Dad. Thanks for dinner," she said without moving.

"Yeah, thanks, Dad," Jessica echoed. She got out of the car and headed for the door.

"Everything OK, Liz?" Mr. Wakefield asked gently.

Elizabeth nodded and reached for the door handle. "Sure, Dad. Good night."

She slid out, then stood on the curb, waving. Her father drove off, and in a moment the tail-lights disappeared around the corner.

"What are you waiting for, Liz?" her sister called from the front porch. "Hurry up, will you."

Sighing, Elizabeth turned and walked up to the house.

Eight

Maria looked out the window of Winston's father's car as they drove through downtown Sweet Valley. "Oh—we're right near the campaign office!" she exclaimed. "Can we stop for a minute?"

"What for? It's Saturday night!" Winston asked in surprise.

"I know, but I accidentally left my history book there the other day, and I have to study tomorrow," Maria said. "I have a test on Monday."

Winston turned the corner and pulled up in front of the office. "Do you think anybody's even there? It looks dark to me."

Maria squinted at the storefront windows. "Well, Liz did say Mr. Wakefield was going to take her and Jessica out to dinner tonight. It's probably useless, but I'll see if the door is locked." She opened the car door and stepped out onto the sidewalk.

"You'd better be fast. Otherwise, I'll have to leave without you," Winston teased.

Maria stuck her tongue out at him and ran to the building. The door was open, but the office seemed to be deserted. Maria looked around. It felt spooky to be there alone. The campaign office had so many unhappy associations for her that just being there made her feel uncomfortable sometimes. She decided not to turn on a light, since she could see well enough from the streetlamp that was right outside the windows. She crossed the room softly to the table she had been using before. Her history book was right where she had left it.

Just as she picked it up, however, the telephone beside her rang. Without thinking, she picked up the receiver.

But before she could answer, another voice said, "Yeah?"

"Knapp, is that you?" asked a man on the other end of the line.

Maria froze. Mr. Knapp was there, too. He had to be in Mr. Wakefield's office. But why? And what was he doing there in the dark? It seemed very odd. Instinctively, she kept silent.

"Yes," Knapp said.

"It's Robertson. Are you alone?"

"Wakefield is out with his kids," Knapp replied in a smug voice. "And then he's working at home on his next speech. He's as happy as a clam."

Robertson laughed, and for some reason the sound gave Maria the shivers. She realized that it was Sy Robertson, a man who had helped out on her father's campaign. He was a local real estate dealer, but that was all Maria knew about him.

"So, how's it going?" Robertson asked. "You're not going to blow it again, are you?"

Knapp snorted. "Come on, give me a little credit. I've got Wakefield where we want him, believe me. He doesn't have the slightest idea what's going on. And when this election is over and he's in office, he'll realize it's time to start returning a few favors. And he'll be perfectly happy to do it, too. He'll think it's the honorable thing to do to repay a loyal supporter. He might even think our plans are for the good of Sweet Valley."

"It's nice to hear you're being more tactful this time," Robertson said. "You went a little overboard before."

"OK, OK," Knapp said. "So I pushed Santelli a little too hard. But we took care of him, and now he's out of the picture. With Wakefield, everything will go smoothly."

Maria almost gasped out loud. Knapp and Robertson had framed her father! And they were trying to use Mr. Wakefield for their own purposes. But what *were* their purposes? That was what she didn't understand.

"Make sure it does," Robertson warned. "I've got a lot riding on that oceanfront project. I don't want anything to go wrong now. The election is only two weeks away. Don't let me down."

"Leave it all to me," Knapp said. "Everything is going just the way I planned it."

Maria's hand was trembling so hard, she was afraid she couldn't hang up without giving herself away. But she put down the receiver carefully, hugged her history book to her chest, and tiptoed out of the office. She closed the door carefully behind her. By the time she climbed into Winston's car, she was shaking all over. She buried her face in her hands and tried to control her feelings.

"What's wrong?" Winston asked. "Maria, are you all right?"

Maria squeezed her eyes shut. All she could think about was how excited and hopeful her father had been about being mayor of Sweet Valley and how devastated he was now. It was all because of Knapp and Robertson. She was so furious that she wanted to scream.

Winston put his arms around her and held her tight. "What? Just try to calm down and tell me. Who was there in the office? What happened?"

"It's awful," Maria whispered. She drew a shuddering breath and told Winston everything she had heard. He was silent until she finished.

"It makes me sick," Winston finally said in a low, intense voice.

"No kidding! I thought I was going to have a heart attack right there," Maria said. "We have to tell everyone what I heard." She looked into Winston's eyes. "I have to clear my father's name. I always knew he was innocent, and this proves it!"

Winston nodded gravely. "Right. But, Maria, listen, you don't have any evidence. If you just accuse them of setting up your dad, nobody will believe you. They'll just think you're a hysterical kid."

"But what else can I do?" Maria pleaded. She groaned and shook her head. "I can't even think straight, I'm so upset!"

"I understand," Winston said, hugging her again. "Let's just try to think logically about what we should do. There has to be a way to get Knapp."

"There is," Maria said fiercely. "I'm going to get him for what he did to my dad. He's going to wish he'd never heard of Sweet Valley by the time I'm done with him."

When Jessica heard a car pull up in front of the house at eleven-thirty, she quickly turned out the overhead light in her bedroom and raced to the window. She saw her mother get out of Mr. Collins's car, wave, and head for the house. "She's home," Jessica announced loudly. She ran through the bathroom to Elizabeth's room. "Mom's home," she repeated.

"So?" Elizabeth said in a sour voice. She was reading in bed. Ever since they had returned from the restaurant, Elizabeth had not said a word to Jessica.

"Liz, don't you hope she had fun with Mr. Collins?" Jessica asked. She knew Elizabeth liked the teacher. What was wrong with his going out with their mother?

Elizabeth turned a page. "You know what my answer is, Jessica."

"Hmm." Jessica sat down on the edge of Elizabeth's bed and scowled at the floor. "I guess it's probably hopeless," she decided. "Tonight was more like a date with Dad than with Mr. Collins."

Elizabeth shot her an irritated look.

Jessica fiddled with the gold lavaliere around

her neck. "So who else do you think Mom would want to go out with?" Jessica asked. She nudged her sister's leg under the covers. "Come on, help me think, Liz."

"Are you out of your mind?" Elizabeth shouted, slamming down her book. "Doesn't it mean anything to you that Mom and Dad were happy being together tonight? Doesn't that matter to you at all?"

Jessica sighed and shook her head. "Sure, it was nice, Liz. But it doesn't change anything."

"But this could be the start of their getting back together," Elizabeth insisted. "If you just leave them alone, they'll work it out!"

"I don't think that's going to happen, I really don't," Jessica said regretfully.

Elizabeth's lower lip trembled. "How can you say that? How can you be so casual about it?" She climbed out of bed and began pacing back and forth across the bedroom. "How can you keep trying to fix Mom up with dates? I think it's really sick!"

Jessica shrugged and leaned back on her elbows. "I just don't want Mom to be lonely, that's all. There's nothing sick about that. You're the one who wants to keep dragging the past around. *That's* sick."

"Why don't you let her decide if she's lonely

or not," Elizabeth said. "She can take care of herself without your help."

"Fine. Forget I ever mentioned it," Jessica replied huffily. She stood up and walked out of the room. She slammed the door shut behind her.

Elizabeth was breathing hard. She stared at the door for a long while after her sister left. Why did Jessica have to be so pushy? She just didn't have any sense of how her actions affected others! When the telephone rang beside her bed, she strode over and snatched it up. "Hello?" she snapped.

"This is Maria. Is that you, Liz?"

Elizabeth let out a sigh and sat down on her bed. "Yeah. Hi, Maria. What's up?"

"I'm sorry to call so late, but I had to tell you something. It's very important."

Frowning, Elizabeth said, "Maria, you sound upset. What happened?"

"I went to the campaign office tonight to pick up a book I left there," Maria began. "I thought nobody was there, but Terry's uncle was."

"Mr. Knapp?" Elizabeth prompted. She began to feel a tingle of worry. "What happened?"

"Well—" Maria drew a deep breath and let it out. She was trying to stay calm. "The phone rang, and I answered it. But Knapp answered it, too, at exactly the same time, and he didn't know I was listening. Basically, Knapp said he framed my father because Dad wouldn't go along with some big scheme he wanted."

Elizabeth felt her stomach turn over. "Maria! I can't believe it. I mean, I can believe it, but—" She broke off, stunned and confused.

"And that's not all," Maria went on. "He was also saying that he's been working on *your* father and that he's going to make your father do certain things once he's elected mayor."

"What?" Elizabeth gasped. Her mind was spinning. "That can't be true! Dad would never let him."

"I know. I don't really understand it, either," Maria went on. "But maybe he's doing something to get your father elected, and if it came out, it would hurt *his* reputation instead of Knapp's."

Elizabeth gulped. "No way, Maria. I can't—" She didn't want to believe what she was hearing. She felt sick to her stomach.

"What I'm saying is that your father doesn't even realize it. That's the whole point," Maria went on. "Don't you see?"

With an effort, Elizabeth forced herself to think clearly. "I have to tell my father," she decided. "Can you tell me exactly what you heard so I can tell him? He's at his apartment working on—"

"Wait," Maria cut in. "Don't tell him yet."

Elizabeth frowned. "Why?"

"Because we don't have any evidence against Knapp," Maria explained. "We have to get something that will prove he's a crook."

"You're right," Elizabeth said slowly. She lowered her voice. "OK. So what do we do next?"

Nine

On Sunday afternoon Elizabeth went to the coffee shop around the corner from the campaign office.

"Liz! Over here!" Maria called. She waved from across the restaurant.

Elizabeth hurried over. Sitting in a booth, having sodas and slices of pie, were Maria, Winston, and Terry Knapp. They all looked excited and nervous.

"Hi," Elizabeth said, sliding into the booth next to Terry. She noticed the look of indignation in his eyes. "Did they tell you?"

Terry nodded grimly. "Yeah. It all fits, too. I used to think Uncle Jim was a pretty nice guy, but in the last couple of years, I've learned that he's not the person I thought he was."

"What do you mean?" Winston prompted.

"He's completely power-hungry," Terry explained. "He thinks he can do anything he wants."

Maria looked disgusted. "Has he ever said anything to you about my father?"

"Well," Terry began slowly, "a few months ago he came over for dinner. And he started bragging about how he was going to make his mark on Sweet Valley. He said if he could just get the city council in his pocket, he'd be the richest man in California."

"But what did he mean, 'get the city council in his pocket'?" Elizabeth said in a low voice. "Did he mean he wants to control them?"

"He wants something approved, I think," Terry went on. He frowned in concentration as he tried to remember.

Maria leaned forward across the table. "What did he want approved? Do you know?"

"Sorry," Terry said. He shook his head. "All I know is it was some kind of big development. It might have been on the beach, but I'm fuzzy on that. I just don't know for sure."

"Robertson mentioned something about an oceanfront project," Maria said. "I wonder if that's what this is all about."

Elizabeth exhaled slowly. "And he's been trying to get my father to talk about economic development for the city in every single speech.

He keeps saying that's what the voters want to hear."

"Sounds like that's what *he* wants to hear," Winston put in. He took another bite of pie.

Maria nodded. "If my dad knew what Mr. Knapp was trying to do and didn't want to go along with it—"

"Then Uncle Jim couldn't afford to let your dad become mayor," Terry finished for her.

"And now he says he's 'taking care' of my father, and Dad doesn't suspect anything," Elizabeth said. She felt a strong surge of protective love for her father. "We have to do something to stop Knapp."

"Knapp, and Robertson, too," Maria reminded her. "I'm convinced they've got some big project that they want approved. So they're using all their influence to get your father elected, and they think once he's in office, he'll be on their side."

Winston tilted his head to one side. "You don't think it could be an oceanfront development right *in* Sweet Valley, do you? I mean, on our beach?"

"No . . ." Maria whispered, shaking her head slowly. But she didn't sound at all sure.

Nobody spoke. The possibility that Knapp was trying to build some kind of development along Sweet Valley's beautiful coastline was frightening.

"OK," Elizabeth said finally. She squared her shoulders. "We have to find some proof that Knapp is using my father."

"And that he framed my father," Maria added.

Winston toyed with his straw. "But what kind of proof? Could we get him to confess? We could hide a tape recorder."

"I don't think that would work," Terry said. "But if he has some big development scheme, don't you think he has to have some plans? I mean, maps and blueprints and stuff?"

"Where would he keep things like that?" Maria asked eagerly.

"His office, I guess," Terry said.

Maria frowned. "If only we could find them."

Elizabeth held up her hand. "But wait—what good would that do? It's not illegal to have maps and plans, you know. We may not want a development in Sweet Valley, but just planning one isn't against the law."

The others were silent.

"It's true," Terry said after a moment. "It wouldn't be proof, but it would show that Knapp and Robertson have an important reason for trying to influence the city government, right?"

"I guess," Elizabeth agreed reluctantly. "But how are we going to find those things?"

Terry and Maria exchanged a significant look. Elizabeth felt her stomach churn as their meaning hit her. "Wait a second," she whispered. "We can't search his office!"

Maria lifted her chin defiantly. "I have to clear my father's name. Don't you want to make sure your dad isn't hurt, too?"

"Yes, but—" Elizabeth hesitated. "I don't know about this . . ."

Winston met her eyes and shrugged. "You have to do what feels right to you, Liz."

"Listen," Terry said in a low voice. He hunched over the table. "I was there the other day. If anyone sees me, I can always say I left something there and went back for it. He's my uncle, nobody would think it was strange if I was there."

"How long do you think it would take?" Maria asked.

"Maybe half an hour? I'm not sure," Terry mused.

Elizabeth listened silently. She was absolutely positive that Knapp was a crook. It seemed pretty clear that he had framed Maria's father to get him out of the way and that he was making sure Mr. Wakefield was in his debt. And it was obvious that the goal Knapp was pursuing would be a disaster for Sweet Valley. So they had a duty to expose him. But breaking into his office and searching it for evidence—that was a pretty drastic step.

"Liz, it's the only way," Maria said. "You don't have to help, but I'm going to do it."

"Me, too," Terry added. "I want to make sure he doesn't get his way on this thing. It could affect my whole family."

Elizabeth looked at her friends. They were willing to take the risk. And if they found something, her father would benefit. She couldn't let them do it alone.

"All right," she said slowly. "I'll go with you. But I think Winston should stay out of it."

"What?" Winston said in surprise.

"I agree," Maria said gravely. "There's no point in your taking the chance of getting caught. I'd feel terrible if you went with us."

"But, Maria—" Winston began.

She shook her head. "I mean it, Win. I don't want you to get more involved than you already are."

He dropped his gaze and nodded.

"Terry, when's a good time for us to get into the office?" Elizabeth asked.

Terry thought about it for a moment, then said, "I think the best time would be tomorrow night, when the office building is still open for the janitors. I know Uncle Jim usually leaves by seven o'clock."

"OK," Elizabeth said with determination. "We'll go tomorrow night."

Jessica was sitting at the big table in the campaign office, lazily checking over voter lists. She was supposed to be making telephone calls to people to remind them to vote, but her mind wasn't on the job. She was too busy thinking about Ramon Valdes, one of her father's political aides. He was sitting at his desk, reading.

She couldn't say for sure, but Jessica guessed he was about her mother's age. He had held several appointed offices in city government. His job on the campaign was to act as a liaison to the Hispanic community in Sweet Valley.

But more importantly, he was attractive and single. Jessica watched him for a few minutes and then made up her mind. He and Mrs. Wakefield would probably hit it off right away. The only reason she hadn't considered him before was because she had had such high hopes for Mr. Collins. But now that potential romance was ancient history, and it was time to try again.

"Hi, Ramon," she said, strolling over to his desk. "What are you working on?"

He looked up as she sat down. "Hi. I'm going over a list of concerns submitted by the North Side Neighborhood Association. It's real politics: what they want, what they'll do for the campaign to get it, that sort of stuff."

"It sounds really fascinating," Jessica said with an admiring smile. "That's the sort of thing my mother would be really interested in hearing about."

"Oh, really?" he asked politely. "I thought she wasn't interested in politics."

Jessica made a face. "That's what everyone thinks, but I'm telling you, she loves it. The only reason she isn't involved in this campaign is . . . well you know."

"I know," Ramon said. "I'm sorry about your parents."

"Oh, don't be!" Jessica jumped in. "They're both so happy with the decision, I can't tell you. Mom just loves being single again." She looked at him earnestly.

"You know, that's very interesting," Ramon said. "I really like being single, too. I can do what I want, go where I want. I know it sounds selfish, but I like not having to check in with anyone about what I'm doing. It's just me and my cats."

Jessica kept a cheerful expression on her face. But inside she was frowning. This wasn't going particularly well. She decided to try a new tack.

"You have cats?" she asked. "My mother loves cats."

Ramon's eyes lit up. "I can't imagine being without mine—they're Siamese. Very finicky, of course, but I like that. They're very dignified, very opinionated. Estrella, that's the female, has such a personality! She has to have everything just the way she likes it, or she gives me the cold shoulder. And Maximillian—he thinks he's the boss at home, let me tell you."

"Oh, really?" Jessica said.

"Yes!" Ramon chuckled. "There was this one time when Estrella decided the only place she wanted to sleep was on my pillow, but—"

"Um, excuse me, I have to get back to work," Jessica cut in quickly, pretending to notice the time. She hurried back to the telephone table.

"What a bore," she said under her breath. Sighing dramatically, she picked up her lists and chose a name to call. In her opinion, the whole campaign was beginning to get tedious. As she picked up the telephone, her gaze moved to the front entrance. Just then, Elizabeth, Maria, and Terry walked in.

Jessica was happy to hang up the phone. Any distraction was welcome.

"Where've you been?" she asked as Elizabeth sat down across from her.

"Nowhere!" Elizabeth said quickly. She knew she couldn't tell Jessica what she had learned and what the plan was. The fewer people who knew, the better it was.

Jessica, however, was convinced Elizabeth was up to something. "Nowhere?" she asked suspiciously.

Elizabeth pulled some voter sheets toward her. "Oh, just at the coffee shop," she said without looking up.

"With Maria and Terry?" Jessica prompted.

Elizabeth nodded. "Yes."

"You could have asked me," Jessica pointed out. *Unless you had a reason for not wanting me along*, she added to herself.

Jessica slumped in her chair and studied her twin's downturned face. "What's going on?" she asked sharply.

"Nothing," Elizabeth said.

Jessica narrowed her eyes. "Nothing? Are you up to something?"

Elizabeth couldn't look at Jessica. "Of course not."

"Yes, you are," Jessica said. "Is it about Mom?"

"No," Elizabeth said and gave a forced laugh. "You're imagining things, Jess."

Jessica smiled knowingly. "Then it's something about Dad, right?"

Elizabeth picked up a telephone and began to punch in a phone number.

Another doomed mission to get Mom and Dad back

together, Jessica thought. She leaned across the table. "Liz, it'll never work," she said in a low voice when Elizabeth completed her call.

Instantly, Elizabeth looked up, an expression of guilt in her eyes. Jessica was surprised to get such a severe reaction.

"What—what do you mean?" Elizabeth stammered.

"They're not going to get back together, Liz. I keep telling you."

"Oh, right," Elizabeth said and smiled weakly. "I guess you're right."

Jessica felt a nagging doubt. Something was definitely up, but she had no idea what.

Ten

Elizabeth, Maria, and Terry huddled under an awning together, watching a steady rain drizzle down around them. The weather matched Elizabeth's mood perfectly. She felt like a criminal, but she had to go through with it. There was too much at stake to back out now.

"OK," she said, hunching her shoulders against the damp breeze, "I'll go in first and distract the guard."

Maria and Terry nodded. Elizabeth drew a deep breath and then made a dash for the entrance of Mr. Knapp's office building.

"Whew!" she said, running inside. She smiled at the guard. "It's really awful outside!"

"What can I do for you this evening, young lady?" he said politely.

Elizabeth shook the rain from her hair. "My

mother is picking me up in a few minutes. Is it all right if I wait for her inside? I was getting soaked out there."

"Sure," the man said. "You're better off waiting in here, where it's nice and dry."

Elizabeth smiled again and breathed a sigh of relief. "Thanks a lot."

She wandered around the big lobby, carefully checking the location of the stairs and the elevator. The guard's station was in the center of the lobby, but toward the rear. The man gave her another friendly smile and started reading a paperback mystery.

Elizabeth kept wandering, and glancing toward the entrance. Through the rain trickling outside the glass, she saw Maria and Terry waiting for her signal.

"Your mother's a little late, huh?" the guard asked.

"It must be the rain," Elizabeth said. She looked outside and then at her watch. The guard went back to his book.

"What are you reading?" Elizabeth asked, walking over and standing to the guard's right.

He had to turn away from the front entrance to speak to her directly. "A real good old-fashioned detective story," he said.

"Oh, can I see it? I think I've read this one," Elizabeth said, leaning forward to look at the title. She frowned. "Yes, this sounds familiar."

104

Behind the guard's back, Maria and Terry slipped inside the front entrance and into the door marked "Stairs." It shut behind them without a sound. Elizabeth relaxed slightly.

"I wonder where my mother is," she said in a worried tone. She began pacing back and forth again.

The guard picked up his telephone. "Why don't you call home and see if she left yet?"

"She's not at home," Elizabeth said. "She was coming on her way from—from exercise class," she improvised. "I guess traffic is probably slow."

She began pacing nervously back and forth again. From time to time, she would stand by the glass doors and look out into the twilight. And she periodically checked her watch. To the guard, it would look like she was waiting for her mother. But in reality, she was timing Terry and Maria. They knew they couldn't risk more than twenty minutes in Knapp's office.

The time was quickly slipping away. Once she strolled aimlessly to the doorway that led upstairs and peeked through the small window. There was no sign of her friends.

What could they be doing? she wondered. Was it a good sign or a bad sign that they were taking a long time? All she knew was that waiting was making her more nervous by the minute. She tensed when the guard set his thermos down with a thump, startling her.

Elizabeth gave him a faint smile and looked out at the street. Then her heart leapt. Mr. Knapp was stepping out of a taxi! He must be on his way to his office!

"Is there a ladies' room I could use?" Elizabeth asked quickly.

"Sure, there's one on the second floor, down the hall on the right," the guard said.

"Thanks." Elizabeth yanked open the door to the stairs and ran up them two at a time. She had to get to her friends before Knapp reached his office.

She was panting by the time she got to the fourth floor. She pulled open the door. One quick glance at the elevator lights told her someone was coming up. Elizabeth sprinted down the hallway, careened around the corner, and burst into room 415.

Maria and Terry whirled around in shock. "Oh, Liz!" Maria gasped. "What—"

"He's coming," Elizabeth told them breathlessly.

Terry went pale and shoved a filing cabinet drawer shut. "What? Right now? We've got to go!"

"There's no time," Elizabeth said. "We have to hide!"

They all looked around wildly. Then Maria pointed. "The closet," she whispered, snapping off the light switch. "Come on."

Without another word, they all piled into the closet on the far side of the office. It was filled with boxes, and there was barely enough room for all of them inside. Elizabeth fought to bring her breathing under control. The slightest sound would give them away.

"I don't think the closet door is completely shut," Terry whispered. "Can you—"

The door of the office opened before anyone could make a move. Elizabeth and the others froze.

The office overhead light was turned on, and a beam slanted in through the crack of the closet door. Elizabeth had a narrow view of the room beyond. Jim Knapp crossed her line of vision and disappeared. They could all hear him take off his coat and shake it out and put something —it sounded like a briefcase—on his desk.

Don't let him hang up his coat, Elizabeth prayed silently.

Knapp sat down at his desk and picked up the telephone. Elizabeth held her breath.

"It's me," Knapp said. "Yeah. No, that's all taken care of. We're in great shape. It's smooth sailing from here on." He paused to listen. "OK," Knapp said with a chuckle. "No, I won't be needing to make any anonymous bank deposits like I did with our friend Santelli."

Maria let out a tiny gasp. Elizabeth's heart almost stopped, but Knapp didn't seem to have heard.

"Fine. That's right. Wakefield has a big speech coming up tomorrow night—that'll be the clincher."

Elizabeth felt a wave of anger and indignation wash over her.

"OK," Knapp concluded. "I'll just make copies of the plans and bring them over so we can present them to the investors. Right. Bye."

Knapp hung up and crossed into Elizabeth's line of vision again. He stooped behind one tall filing cabinet and pulled something out from behind it. It was a large file folder, bulky with papers. He opened it on the desk, searched through it methodically, and pulled out several sheets. Then he went to the photocopying machine and ran off some copies. Elizabeth could see the satisfied look on his face, and it made her furious.

In a few moments, Knapp returned the original documents to the file, hid it again, and put the copies in his briefcase. Then he put on his raincoat, hit the lights, and left.

The closet was pitch dark again.

"Wow," Maria breathed.

Elizabeth cringed as she moved her stiffened muscles. They stepped quietly out of the closet, and Terry fumbled for the light switch.

"That was close," Elizabeth said. "But I saw something."

The others looked at her expectantly. "What? We didn't find a thing."

Elizabeth went to the filing cabinet and reached behind it. When she pulled out the hidden file, her friends looked shocked.

"You know it's fishy if he has to hide it," Terry said.

"Let's see what's in it," Maria said, moving to the desk.

Terry and Maria looked over Elizabeth's shoulder as she opened the file. There were letters with "Knapp Development Corporation" across the top, and pages of cost estimates and market analyses. When Elizabeth turned over another sheet and found a rough sketch of a boardwalk with arcades and shops, Maria caught her breath.

"That's our beach," she said in an outraged voice. She jabbed one finger at the drawing. "Look at that lighthouse on the point there, and those buoys. That's what you see from the beach."

"You're right," Elizabeth whispered.

"Well, we knew he was planning something like this," Terry pointed out. "I'll make copies of these while you look through the rest of the papers."

He turned on the copy machine and got to work. Elizabeth and Maria sorted carefully through the rest of the file. Mostly it was straight-forward business information. They couldn't be sure if it was all legitimate or not. But then they found a bank receipt, tucked between two sheets of computer printout.

"What is this?" Elizabeth asked, turning it over.

"It's a receipt for a teller's check for ten thousand dollars," Maria read. She looked up swiftly and met Elizabeth's eyes. "That's how much was deposited in my father's private account."

"The so-called bribe," Elizabeth added. She examined the receipt. "Look! Someone wrote in a number along the side. It looks like it's an account number," she said.

"I have no idea if that's my dad's account number," Maria said. "I wouldn't be surprised if it was, though. I'd bet anything Knapp put that money in Dad's account to make it look like a bribe."

"We'll make a copy of that, too," Elizabeth said. She glanced at her watch. "We really have to go—we've been here too long already."

"I'm done," Terry said.

Maria made a copy of the canceled check, and they restored the file to its hiding place.

After a quick check to see if the office looked all right, they turned out the light and hurried down the stairwell.

"I'll go out first and distract the guard again," Elizabeth whispered. She paused for a moment to compose herself and then opened the door.

"I thought we were going to have to send a search party after you," the guard joked as Elizabeth walked out into the lobby.

"Well, the second floor ladies' room was locked," Elizabeth replied, "so I had to go up another flight, and then the cleaning people were there—"

"That's OK, I'm just teasing," he said.

Elizabeth glanced at the doorway to the stairs. She could see Maria and Terry waiting for her to give them a chance to escape.

"Is there a back door to this building?" Elizabeth asked, walking past the guard. "I wonder if my mother is at the wrong entrance."

The guard turned around to look at her. "Nope—there's just this one, plus the fire escapes."

From the corner of her eye, Elizabeth saw Maria and Terry sneak out the front door. She breathed a sigh of relief.

"Well, I don't know where my mother could be," Elizabeth said irritably. She strode to the entrance and looked out. "Oh! There's her car! Thanks so much. Bye-bye!"

She hurried out into the rain and chased after her friends.

"We did it!" Maria said. Her eyes shone with excitement.

Terry nodded. "We sure did. Now what do we do?"

"I vote we go to the police," Maria said in a firm voice.

"No," Terry argued, "I think we should call Uncle Jim and tell him we know everything. Then he'll have to lay off."

Elizabeth made a skeptical face. "I don't think we can scare him off that easily. And the thing is, we don't really know where we stand with this stuff. We don't even know if what Knapp has done is illegal. None of us is a legal expert."

"We need a lawyer," Terry said.

Maria looked at Elizabeth, and then Terry glanced her way, too. "How about your father?" Maria suggested. "He's tied up in this, too. He'll know what to do."

"I guess," Elizabeth said slowly. She brushed a raindrop off her cheek and nodded. "OK. I'll take the stuff over to Dad's apartment right now."

Eleven

Elizabeth knocked once on the door of Mr. Wakefield's apartment. She wished there was some way of sparing her father what she had to tell him. But there was no way to avoid giving him the bad news.

The door opened suddenly. "Hey, Liz!" Mr. Wakefield exclaimed happily. "Come on in, honey. This is a nice surprise."

"Hi, Dad," Elizabeth replied in a subdued tone. She followed him in.

"You're just in time," her father said, moving briskly across the room to his desk. "I need an audience, and you're just the ticket. Tomorrow's the big night—I haven't debated since law school. Let me try out some of my proposals on you."

Elizabeth couldn't bear to hear the enthusiasm in his voice. He was so excited, and he was about to receive a slap in the face.

"Oh—and another bit of good news came in today," he went on, smiling like a kid. "The editors at the *Sweet Valley News* announced today that they're endorsing my candidacy. Isn't that fantastic?"

"That's great, Dad," Elizabeth said weakly.

Mr. Wakefield went into his small kitchen. "Let me get you some juice or sparkling water first," he said. "I'm afraid I don't have any soft drinks. How about—"

"Dad!" Elizabeth broke in.

He popped around the corner again and gave her an inquisitive look. "Yes?"

"Dad, I—" She stopped.

Mr. Wakefield's smile wavered. "Is something wrong, Liz?"

Nodding, Elizabeth sank onto the couch. "Dad, I have to tell you something, and it's pretty important."

"Go ahead," he urged, sitting across from her. "I'm listening."

Elizabeth licked her lips. "Dad, Maria overheard Mr. Knapp talking on the phone the other day. She heard him say some pretty"—she searched for the right word—"some pretty incredible things."

Her father frowned. "What things? If it's some-

114

thing you think I should know, don't be afraid to tell me, honey. Just go ahead."

"OK," Elizabeth agreed. She took a deep breath, but she couldn't look at her father. "He was talking to Mr. Robertson, and they were saying that a big development plan they've been working on for the beach is sure to get approved because they'll have influence with the city government after the election."

Mr. Wakefield nodded silently.

"And that this time there wouldn't be any hitches like there were with Mr. Santelli. They said they had to take care of Mr. Santelli because he wasn't going along with them."

Elizabeth raised her eyes to her father's face. He was regarding her in complete silence, hardly moving a muscle.

"They said that they were being more careful this time," Elizabeth went on. "And that you didn't suspect anything . . ." She wanted to go on but her voice gave out. Elizabeth handed her father the documents she had been clutching in her hand. He took them without a word and began reading them.

The silence stretched out unbearably. Elizabeth twisted her hands together in her lap. She had never seen her father look angrier. It was frightening.

"Maybe I misunderstood it all," she suggested

in a hopeless tone. "Maybe I'm just blowing this all out of proportion."

Her father raised his hand to cut her off. Elizabeth blinked back tears. She felt responsible for the pain and anger and humiliation she knew he must be feeling now.

"What is this bank check receipt?" he asked, his voice hard.

"It's the money—that Mr. Santelli was accused of taking as a bribe," she said, faltering. "At least, that's what we figured. Mr. Knapp wrote in a number along the side. Maria is checking her father's account number at home."

Mr. Wakefield held up the papers. "Where did you get these, Elizabeth?"

"Mr. Knapp's office," Elizabeth confessed. "I had to—"

Her father sat back and let out a heavy sigh. "This is unbelievable," he said. "Do you realize what you've done?"

"Yes," Elizabeth whispered.

"Oh, Liz." Mr. Wakefield shook his head.

"I'm sorry I let you down, Dad," Elizabeth choked out. "But I had to find some proof. He's a crook and he's using you. Don't you see?"

"I do, Liz," he said sadly. "I understand that you did it because you thought I was in trouble. And I know you couldn't have made that decision lightly."

"I didn't," she agreed.

"But I don't know what to do now," he went on, almost as though he were talking to himself. "I just don't know what to do."

Elizabeth nodded, but she couldn't speak.

"I can't trust anybody anymore. I don't know who's involved in this," he said painfully. "I don't know whom to trust."

"How about Mom?" Elizabeth said quietly. She held her breath.

"Alice," he said, closing his eyes.

Elizabeth stood up, feeling bolder and more hopeful suddenly. "Let's go home. You can talk to Mom about it—she'll be able to help."

Her father sat where he was for a moment. Then he nodded. "OK."

"Come on, let's go now," Elizabeth urged, taking his hand. She tugged him to his feet and led him to the door. He put his coat on mechanically. Then they left the apartment together.

Outside, it was still raining, and they hurried to Mr. Wakefield's car. Mr. Wakefield started the car and drove slowly. The windshield wipers clicked back and forth, casting moving shadows from oncoming headlights. Neither Elizabeth nor her father spoke.

Before long, Mr. Wakefield turned the car down their street and came to a stop in front of the house. The lights were on, and Mrs. Wakefield's car was in the driveway.

Elizabeth ran through the rain to the front door and burst inside. "Mom?" she called out.

"I'm in the kitchen."

"Can you come here?" Elizabeth asked, glancing back through the door. Her father was coming slowly up the walk, oblivious to the rain. "It's important!"

Her parents both reached the hall at the same time. Mrs. Wakefield stopped in surprise.

"Ned. What—" She stopped and took a step forward. "What *happened?*" she asked, noticing his stricken expression. "Did something happen to Jessica? She went over to Lila's house and—"

He shook his head. "No. It's not Jessica. It's something else."

"Come in," Alice said, closing the door. "You look terrible."

"I feel terrible," he agreed, going into the living room. He took off his coat and draped it over a chair. Then he began to tell Mrs. Wakefield what Elizabeth had told him. Elizabeth sat next to him, filling in the gaps in the story. Her mother perched on the arm of the couch, listening quietly.

"Now what?" she asked when he was finished.

"I don't know, Alice," he said, shaking his head. He let his breath out slowly. "I thought I could make a difference for the city. But now I know it was all one big lie from beginning to end. How can I go on with it now?"

Mrs. Wakefield crossed to his side. "Don't say that, Ned. You have to go on. You have more integrity and more heart to give this city than anyone else. You can't let this stop you."

"I'm just as guilty as Knapp and Robertson," he said fiercely. "I *let* them influence me! Sweet Valley doesn't need an idiot for a mayor."

"Dad—" Elizabeth began. She looked imploringly at her mother.

"Ned, you can expose Knapp and go on with the campaign," Mrs. Wakefield insisted. "The voters will understand if you lay it all out for them. They'll know you had nothing to do with this scheme."

He shook his head. "There would always be a doubt in people's minds. I can't live with that on my conscience."

"You don't have a thing in this world to feel guilty about!" Mrs. Wakefield insisted.

"How about calling a press conference?" Elizabeth offered. "Tell everyone what you know."

"That would only land me with a whopping lawsuit for slander," her father said.

"Listen, Ned," Mrs. Wakefield went on, taking his hand. "You've got evidence—take it to the police. That detective we met last year. What was his name—Cabrini? Call him, show him what you've got."

"It's not admissible," Mr. Wakefield told her. He looked at Elizabeth and smiled regretfully. "Evidence obtained without a search warrant can't be used in court."

Elizabeth felt her chin quiver. "I'm sorry, Dad."

"No, honey, it's not your fault," he said quickly. "If you hadn't done it, we never would have known until it was too late."

Mrs. Wakefield looked over the documents again. "If you told Detective Cabrini what Maria heard on the telephone, wouldn't that be enough to convince a judge to issue a search warrant?"

"It's hearsay," Mr. Wakefield said. He sat forward and frowned. "And she isn't exactly an impartial witness, either. But if I say it's a reliable anonymous source . . ."

"They'd find the same things we did," Elizabeth put in. "Just make sure the detective knows to look behind the filing cabinets for the folder."

"It's enough to discredit him, at the very least," Alice Wakefield said. "He'll never get his plans admitted for consideration if he can be shown to have used influence this way."

"You're right," Ned agreed. "But I want him

on the Santelli frame-up, too. If Cabrini can link the check to Jim Knapp—"

"It exceeds the legal limit for a political contribution, right?" Elizabeth interrupted.

Her father nodded. "But that doesn't prove Santelli had no knowledge of it. We have to figure a way of working this all out."

"Maybe . . ." Mrs. Wakefield began. She looked down at her lap and frowned thoughtfully.

"What?" Ned asked.

"Tomorrow night—at the big rally," Mrs. Wakefield said slowly. "Maybe there's something you can do about Knapp then."

Elizabeth looked at her parents and tried hard to contain her emotions. This was the way things used to be between them. Suddenly, she felt she had to leave the room. If she stayed, she knew she would start to cry.

"I'll be right back," she whispered, slipping out of the living room. She went into the kitchen and poured herself some juice.

This was the end of the separation, she was sure. Her parents would stay up late, discussing what Mr. Wakefield should do, and in the process, they would realize how much they still loved each other and how much they needed to be together. Her father would come home to stay, Elizabeth could feel it.

She wondered what was being said in the

other room. Part of her wanted to give her parents privacy. But another part of her couldn't wait to know. She walked quietly back to the living room door.

"Thanks," her father was saying in a low voice. "I don't know what I would have done if I couldn't talk to you about it."

"That's all right," Alice said.

They were silent.

Then Mr. Wakefield stood up. "Well, I guess I should be going—"

"Right, the weather . . ."

"Well, good night, Alice."

Mrs. Wakefield stood up. "Good night, Ned. I'll see you tomorrow. Good luck."

Elizabeth heard their footsteps go out into the hallway, and then she heard the front door close.

Twelve

The following evening Elizabeth and her mother drove to City Hall together. It took several minutes to find a parking space, since downtown Sweet Valley was mobbed for the big pre-election rally.

"I wonder if Jessica is here already?" Elizabeth asked nervously. Jessica and the other varsity cheerleaders were part of the celebration.

City Hall was swathed in red, white, and blue banners, American flags, and California state flags. The mobs of people gathered at the base of the broad steps were talking excitedly, buying balloons, and holding their children on their shoulders. Elizabeth took some mental notes for a newspaper article.

But her mind was really on only one thing: What was her father going to do?

"There's your father," Mrs. Wakefield said, her eyes brightening.

Elizabeth stood on tiptoe. "Where? Oh—I see him. Dad!" She yelled and waved her arms, but he obviously couldn't hear her.

Mr. Wakefield and the other candidates for mayor and city council were on the top step, talking. While she watched, Jim Knapp walked out of the building and began shaking hands. He had a smug, satisfied smile on his face.

Elizabeth held her breath when she saw that her father had noticed him. With a broad smile that would have fooled anybody, Ned Wakefield shook Knapp's hand and said something Elizabeth had no chance of hearing.

"What is he going to do, do you know?" Elizabeth asked her mother.

Alice shook her head. "I'm not sure, Liz. We'll just wait and see. Oh, look—there's Jess."

The cheerleading squad ran up the steps and began leading the crowd through a familiar cheer. Jessica looked on top of the world. She loved being the center of attention. After the crowd was completely revved up, the cheerleaders ran off, and the current mayor stepped up to the microphone.

"Ladies and gentlemen, boys and girls!" he yelled.

The crowd burst into applause. He had been Sweet Valley's mayor for many years, and everyone liked him a lot. He was retiring to run an orange grove.

"Thanks, one and all!" he said. "This is an exciting and important night for Sweet Valley. For the first time in this campaign, all of the candidates are assembled in one place to air their views, ask for your support, and answer to you, the good people of Sweet Valley, California!"

More cheers and applause interrupted him, and he waved his hands for silence. "It's wonderful to see so many of you here tonight. I know you all care about this wonderful city of ours as much as I do."

"Did Dad go to the police?" Elizabeth asked her mother in a low voice as she kept her eyes on her father.

"I think so, but I don't know what the outcome was," Mrs. Wakefield answered. "I guess we'll know pretty soon."

Just then the mayor introduced Mr. Wakefield as the first candidate. The crowd applauded loudly, and some people cheered. Elizabeth felt herself tingling with excitement.

"Thank you, fellow citizens of Sweet Valley," Ned Wakefield began.

He waited for the applause to die down before he went on. "I'm glad for the chance to talk to so many of you this evening. I want to share some of my thoughts about Sweet Valley with you. This city has been wonderful to me. My children have grown up here, and my wife and I have both worked here and felt supported by this wonderful community. There's something special about Sweet Valley, and you all know that."

Everyone applauded, and there were whistles and cheers. Elizabeth was so proud of her father that she couldn't stop smiling.

"Unfortunately, those fine qualities that make Sweet Valley so special, and that attract so many wonderful people here, also attract some not so fine people. Some people who want to take advantage of Sweet Valley's charm, beauty, and community spirit. Those who would exploit this town if we gave them the opportunity."

Elizabeth searched the crowd quickly for Jim Knapp. She glimpsed him at the foot of the steps and noticed that his expression was one of wary surprise.

"I know—you think it couldn't happen here. And we want to believe that economic development will always progress sanely and sensibly in Sweet Valley. But unless we are sharp enough to spot sharks among us, we'll be gobbled up like so many other towns in California."

The crowd had grown quiet. Elizabeth strained to see over everyone's heads.

"One person in particular," her father went on. "One person in particular has been masquerading as a friend to us all. But in reality, he has been planning to exploit the city. Yet there's another side to this story. There was one man who knew what was going on: He saw behind the false promises and the comfortable lies, and he refused to play the game. He suffered for it, ladies and gentlemen. He suffered terribly." He paused dramatically and then added, "I'm talking about Peter Santelli. He paid the ultimate price for decency and integrity in this city."

A puzzled murmur rippled through the crowd.

"He wouldn't play the game," Mr. Wakefield shouted, pounding his fist on the podium. "It's a dirty game, and sometimes you don't even know you're in it. I have been in it myself throughout my campaign, and I didn't know I was only a pawn, being manipulated by someone craftier than myself."

Elizabeth regarded James Knapp. He looked furious—and frightened. He began to weave his way casually but steadily through the press of onlookers.

"Mom, there he goes," Elizabeth hissed. Without waiting for an answer, she slipped through the crowd to follow him.

"Well, let me tell you," she heard her father say, "I refuse to be manipulated by people who only want to use Sweet Valley for their own ends. I won't let anyone ever say that Ned Wakefield is tainted by dirty politics."

Elizabeth could see Knapp put on speed, and she quickened her pace, too. She maneuvered through the mob as quickly as she could. Up ahead, Knapp began to run, and he turned a corner out of sight.

"No!" Elizabeth gasped, pushing and shoving in earnest. She raced after him and skidded around the corner.

Then she stopped in her tracks. Jim Knapp was having his rights read to him by Detective Cabrini.

"I'm calling my lawyer," Knapp was exclaiming.

"You get one phone call at the station, courtesy of the taxpayers of Sweet Valley," Cabrini told Knapp. He pointed into the car. "Please take a seat."

Elizabeth watched in amazement as the detective drove off with Knapp. They had actually stopped him, after all!

Another burst of applause reminded her that

her father was still speaking. The crowd's enthusiasm was at a fever pitch now. Elizabeth ran back to hear him finish.

"My friends!" he said hoarsely, trying to quiet them. "I want you to know that I will never give you reason to doubt my motives or my decisions—"

"Yeah!" yelled an admiring supporter.

"Because I'm withdrawing from the race," Mr. Wakefield said.

The crowd hushed.

"What?" Elizabeth whispered.

"I'm sorry," he said, shaking his head. "I can't go on with honor."

The whole audience was still, shocked into silence. Then, very slowly, one person began to clap. Then another joined in, and another, and soon everyone was clapping and stamping their feet and cheering. The applause was thunderous.

Then Elizabeth saw Mr. Wakefield stride purposefully down the steps. One person was shoving a way through the crowd to him, and Elizabeth's heart soared when she saw it was her mother. Her parents met in a fierce embrace.

Elizabeth was smiling and crying all at once.

On election night the campaign office was feverish with excitement. Everyone was there, and everything was the same, except for one important difference: The "Elect Ned Wakefield" posters had been replaced with ones reading, "Elect Peter Santelli." Since Maria's father had reentered the race, public support for his campaign had been overwhelming. Knapp had confessed in order to throw as much of the blame as possible onto Robertson, and Santelli had been declared completely innocent.

"Isn't this wild?" Jessica said to Elizabeth, sipping a glass of soda. "It's so exciting!"

Elizabeth nodded. But her eyes never left her parents. After all the heartache and anxiety of their separation, she couldn't believe she was seeing them together again. While she watched, her father said something that made her mother laugh. Then they kissed.

"You look positively mushy," Jessica teased.

"Well, aren't you happy?" Elizabeth demanded.

Her sister laughed. "Of course I am. What do you think I am, crazy?"

"I don't think I'll answer that," Elizabeth said happily.

"Hey, Maria!" Jessica called as their friend passed.

Maria changed course and bounced to a halt in front of them. "Hi, guys!" She grinned.

"When do the results start coming in?" Jessica asked. "I mean, when is this officially going to be a victory celebration?"

Maria giggled. "Don't say that—it'll put a jinx on the election," she said.

"It'll be pretty soon," Terry said, joining them.

"Listen up, everyone!" Mr. Wakefield called. He was standing on a chair with a telephone in his hand. "The first voting precinct just called in. Santelli for mayor with fifty-seven percent of the vote!"

Everyone screamed with triumph. Elizabeth and Jessica jumped up and down with excitement. Then Jessica hugged Terry Knapp, which made him look startled and pleased. Elizabeth was smiling so hard, her face hurt.

"Here's another precinct reporting!" Ramon Valdes announced over the clamor. "Third precinct counts sixty-one percent for Santelli."

Soon the noise level had risen so high that Elizabeth could hardly hear herself think. She crossed the crowded room to her mother's side and kissed her.

"This is a great night," she said. "I wouldn't miss it for the world."

Mrs. Wakefield smiled. "Same here," she said.

A lump rose in Elizabeth's throat. She was so happy, she didn't know what to say. "Oh, Mom!" she gasped, putting her arms around her mother.

131

"Hey, is this a private hug, or can anyone join in?" Mr. Wakefield asked.

"Come on," Elizabeth said and laughed.

"Hey, make room for me," Jessica said behind them.

All four of them hugged in a long, tight embrace.

Elizabeth brought her tray over to a table full of people the next day at lunchtime. "Is there room for me?" she asked cheerfully.

"Sure, Liz," Maria said. She shoved Winston's chair. "Scoot over."

Elizabeth squeezed in at the crowded table and grinned at everyone. "How does it feel to be a member of Sweet Valley's first family?" she asked Maria.

"Fabulous!" Maria said.

"You're a political celebrity," Aaron Dallas teased.

"Not only that, but she'll be able to ace the politics and government section in social studies," Enid Rollins put in.

Elizabeth giggled and snapped open her soda can.

"You look happy, Liz," Enid went on.

"It's sick, isn't it?" Todd said, joining the

132

group. He gave Elizabeth a kiss on the cheek. "You look like you just won the lottery."

Elizabeth couldn't stop smiling. "I'm happy because my father is moving back home this afternoon," she announced.

"That's great!" Maria said warmly. "And it's so romantic, too. I mean, your parents must have realized how much they love each other."

"It *is* romantic," Olivia Davidson agreed.

"Look out," Winston said with a groan. "The girls are getting gushy."

Maria blew her straw wrapper at him.

"Congratulations, Liz," Dana Larson said.

Elizabeth's smile faltered a little bit. Dana looked so downcast that Elizabeth was taken off guard. "Thanks . . ." she began awkwardly.

"Don't you think it's romantic, Dana?" Maria asked.

Dana sat back and said cynically, "I don't believe in romance," she said. Dana, who was the lead singer for Sweet Valley High's most popular band, The Droids, was prone to dramatic statements.

"Come on, you don't mean that," Enid said gently.

Dana pretended to be surprised. "I don't? That's news to me."

Todd glanced over at Elizabeth, and she gave him a rueful look.

"Don't you believe in love?" Elizabeth asked her.

Dana took a long drink of soda before answering. "No. I don't," she declared with finality.

Elizabeth was surprised. She wondered if there was a way to convince Dana that she was wrong.

Can Elizabeth change Dana's mind about love? Find out in Sweet Valley High #68, **THE LOVE BET.**

COULD *YOU* BE THE NEXT SWEET VALLEY READER OF THE MONTH?

ENTER BANTAM BOOKS' SWEET VALLEY CONTEST & SWEEPSTAKES IN ONE!

Calling all Sweet Valley Fans! Here's a chance to appear in a Sweet Valley book!

We know how important Sweet Valley is to you. That's why we've come up with a Sweet Valley celebration offering exciting opportunities to have YOUR thoughts printed in a Sweet Valley book!

"How do I become a Sweet Valley Reader of the Month?"

It's easy. Just write a one-page essay (no more than 150 words, please) telling us a little about yourself, and why you like to read Sweet Valley books. We will pick the best essays and print them along with the winner's photo in the back of upcoming Sweet Valley books. Every month there will be a new Sweet Valley High Reader of the Month!

And, there's more!

Just sending in your essay makes you eligible for the Grand Prize drawing for a trip to Los Angeles, California! This once-in-a-life-time trip includes round-trip airfare, accommodations for 5 nights (economy double occupancy), a rental car, and meal allowances. (Approximate retail value: $4,500.)

Don't wait! Write your essay today.
No purchase necessary. See the next page for Official rules.

ENTER BANTAM BOOKS' SWEET VALLEY READER OF THE MONTH SWEEPSTAKES

☐	27650	**AGAINST THE ODDS #51**	$2.95
☐	27720	**WHITE LIES #52**	$2.95
☐	27771	**SECOND CHANCE #53**	$2.95
☐	27856	**TWO BOY WEEKEND #54**	$2.95
☐	27915	**PERFECT SHOT #55**	$2.95
☐	27970	**LOST AT SEA #56**	$2.95
☐	28079	**TEACHER CRUSH #57**	$2.95
☐	28156	**BROKEN HEARTS #58**	$2.95
☐	28193	**IN LOVE AGAIN #59**	$2.95
☐	28264	**THAT FATAL NIGHT #60**	$2.95
☐	28317	**BOY TROUBLE #61**	$2.95
☐	28352	**WHO'S WHO #62**	$2.95
☐	28385	**THE NEW ELIZABETH #63**	$2.95
☐	28487	**THE GHOST OF TRICIA MARTIN #64**	$2.95
☐	28518	**TROUBLE AT HOME #65**	$2.95
☐	28555	**WHO'S TO BLAME #66**	$2.95
☐	28611	**THE PARENT PLOT #67**	$2.95
☐	28618	**THE LOVE BET #68**	$2.95

Buy them at your local bookstore or use this page to order.

☐	15681-0	**TEAMWORK #27**	$2.75
☐	15688-8	**APRIL FOOL! #28**	$2.75
☐	15695-0	**JESSICA AND THE BRAT ATTACK #29**	$2.75
☐	15715-9	**PRINCESS ELIZABETH #30**	$2.75
☐	15727-2	**JESSICA'S BAD IDEA #31**	$2.75
☐	15747-7	**JESSICA ON STAGE #32**	$2.75
☐	15753-1	**ELIZABETH'S NEW HERO #33**	$2.75
☐	15766-3	**JESSICA, THE ROCK STAR #34**	$2.75
☐	15772-8	**AMY'S PEN PAL #35**	$2.75
☐	15778-7	**MARY IS MISSING #36**	$2.75
☐	15779-5	**THE WAR BETWEEN THE TWINS #37**	$2.75
☐	15789-2	**LOIS STRIKES BACK #38**	$2.75
☐	15798-1	**JESSICA AND THE MONEY MIX-UP #39**	$2.75
☐	15806-6	**DANNY MEANS TROUBLE #40**	$2.75
☐	15810-4	**THE TWINS GET CAUGHT $41**	$2.75

Bantam Books, Dept. SVT5, 414 East Golf Road, Des Plaines, IL 60016

Please send me the items I have checked above. I am enclosing $_____
(please add $2.00 to cover postage and handling). Send check or money
order, no cash or C.O.D.s please.

Mr/Ms _____

Address _____

City/State _____ Zip _____

SVT5-9/90

Please allow four to six weeks for delivery.
Prices and availability subject to change without notice.